Vow
of
Vengeance

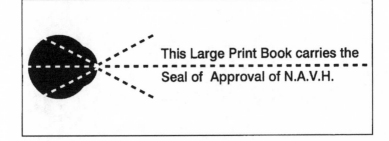

This Large Print Book carries the
Seal of Approval of N.A.V.H.

Vow
of
Vengeance

Lewis B. Patten

Thorndike Press • Waterville, Maine

Published in 2004 by arrangement with
Golden West Literary Agency.

Thorndike Press® Large Print Western.

The tree indicium is a trademark of Thorndike Press.

The text of this Large Print edition is unabridged.
Other aspects of the book may vary from the original edition.

Set in 16 pt. Plantin by Elena Picard.

Printed in the United States on permanent paper.

Library of Congress Cataloging-in-Publication Data

Patten, Lewis B.
    Vow of vengeance / by Lewis B. Patten.
      p. cm.
    ISBN 0-7862-7115-9 (lg. print : hc : alk. paper)
    1. Women pioneers — Fiction. 2. Lynching — Fiction.
3. Wyoming — Fiction. 4. Revenge — Fiction. 5. Widows
— Fiction. 6. Large type books. I. Title.
PS3566.A79V69 2004
   813′.54—dc22   2004059805

Vow
of
Vengeance

As the Founder/CEO of NAVH, the only national health agency solely devoted to those who, although not totally blind, have an eye disease which could lead to serious visual impairment, I am pleased to recognize Thorndike Press* as one of the leading publishers in the large print field.

Founded in 1954 in San Francisco to prepare large print textbooks for partially seeing children, NAVH became the pioneer and standard setting agency in the preparation of large type.

Today, those publishers who meet our standards carry the prestigious "Seal of Approval" indicating high quality large print. We are delighted that Thorndike Press is one of the publishers whose titles meet these standards. We are also pleased to recognize the significant contribution Thorndike Press is making in this important and growing field.

Lorraine H. Marchi, L.H.D.
Founder/CEO
NAVH

* Thorndike Press encompasses the following imprints: Thorndike, Wheeler, Walker and Large Print Press.

Chapter 1

What made it doubly terrible was the suddenness with which it happened. At one instant they were sitting peacefully at the supper table, Sam Dunson and his wife Prudence, eating their quiet supper, and the next instant there was the pound of hoofs entering the yard, and a harsh and brutal yell, "Sam Dunson! Come out of there!"

Sam got to his feet. He laid his napkin on the table and went to the door. There was yet no fear in him in spite of the harshness and urgency of the summons. He opened the door and squinted into the darkness, seeing the dim shapes of horsemen in the yard, recognizing but one of them, Silas Shawcroft in the front.

Sam was thirty, five feet eleven inches tall, with powerful shoulders and a deep, strong chest. His hands were big, calloused from work, and his skin was dark, beginning already to show wrinkles at the corners of his eyes from twelve hours' daily exposure to sun and wind.

This was Wyoming Territory, a land of endless, rolling plains and waving grass. This piece of land was a quarter section, a hundred and sixty acres that would belong to him and Prudence in the fall when they had finished proving up on it. They finally had a total of forty acres plowed, and next spring would plant it all in corn. God would decide whether there would be sufficient rain to make the corn mature.

If it didn't, they would survive anyhow. Prudence had a garden and Sam had ten head of cattle — five cows, four calves, and a bull. They had lived on antelope meat ever since their arrival and they could go on doing so.

He stepped farther out into the yard so that he could better see the horsemen there. For the first time, uneasiness plagued him and made him wish he had picked up his rifle as he left the house. He said, "I'm out. What can I do for you?"

Something heavy and sodden hit the ground at his feet. He knew instantly what it was. Shawcroft's harsh voice said, "You can bring that steer back to life!"

Now he knew how deadly serious this was. But he hadn't killed any beef, his own or anyone else's, since he'd been here, and he hadn't killed the critter to which this soggy hide belonged. He asked, "Where did that come from?"

"Two, three miles southwest of here, where you butchered it. Wagon tracks led right straight here. By God, we've put up with you nesters killin' our beef long enough. It's time some of you paid up."

There was a chorus of shouts behind Shawcroft, as if all of the men were working themselves up to what they meant to do. Sam counted. There were seven of them in all, and now he felt a cold ball of fear lying like something undigested in his gut. This was a lynch mob and they figured on killing him before they left. Not for something he had done but for something they said he'd done. Chances were every one of them knew he hadn't butchered the beef they said he had. It was only an excuse. They wanted him and Prudence off this land and this was the way they were going to accomplish it.

But he'd sell out dearly if he could. He whirled and lunged for the door, seeing Prudence standing just inside, her face white and terror-stricken. Prudence was five months pregnant but as yet it hardly showed.

A rope sailed out, its loop dropping over Sam Dunson's head. He hit the end of it so hard it nearly broke his neck. For an instant it cut off all air from his lungs.

He struck the ground on his back, hands clawing at the rope. His neck was rope-burned, but he was too mad now to even notice that.

The horseman who had roped him backed his horse enough to keep Sam from loosening the rope. Choking, fighting for air, he heard someone yell, "Look out."

Suddenly the rope went slack. He clawed the loop off and struggled to his feet. Prudence was now just outside the door, and she had the rifle in her hands. She jacked a cartridge in and raised the gun.

She never got a chance to shoot. A horse, spurred and galloping, struck her with his shoulder and slammed her bodily against the house. The gun clattered to the ground and one of the men dismounted and picked it up. He emptied it by jacking the lever half a dozen times, then flung it away into the darkness.

Prudence lay slumped against the wall of the house. Shawcroft's harsh voice said, "Burn it! Burn everything!"

Dunson ran toward his wife. He never reached her because once more the rope

10

sailed out and settled over his head.

This time it dropped below the level of his shoulders, effectively pinning his arms to his sides, once more yanking him off his feet. And a shocked horror came to him. Prudence was hurt and he was going to die. Nothing could stop it now.

He was dragged around and around the house, the rider shouting gleefully. His shirt shredded and was torn from him. His underwear suffered a similar fate. Skin was scraped off arms and back and chest. His eyes and nose and mouth filled with dust until he was blinded, choking, unable to breathe. Shawcroft's roar halted the dragging. "Stop it! I don't want him killed that way!"

Prudence suddenly began to scream. The marauders may have thought her screams were from terror, but Sam Dunson knew his wife better than that. Her screams were screams of pain. They had hurt her when they slammed her against the house. Five months pregnant she was, and only God knew what the consequences of that blow were going to be.

Stubbornly, filled with rage, but blinded and helpless, Sam made it to his feet again. He wanted to get the rope off, but every time he tried, the man who had roped him yanked him back. Finally he stopped trying and stood spread-legged, knuckling his dirt-filled eyes, trying to see again.

Shawcroft now said, "Prop up that wagon tongue."

So that was how it was going to be. They were going to hang him from his own wagon tongue. He croaked, "My wife! For God's sake, let me go to my wife!"

Shawcroft said, "Let him."

The rope went slack and Sam Dunson threw it off. Blinking his streaming eyes, he stumbled toward the square of light that marked the door.

Already smoke was pouring from the house. He could see tongues of flame behind the smoke, but he didn't care now about the house. He knelt at Prudence's side and put his arms around her and held her close to him. Her screams had stopped. Now she moaned at intervals as if she were having labor pains. Between them she cried out, "Oh God, Sam, what do they want?"

"They said I killed a beef."

"You didn't!"

"I know it, but they say I did."

"What are they going to do?"

"They're going to kill me, Prue."

She stared at him speechlessly. He could

see her better now. His eyes still burned and tears still streamed from them, but he could see. He said, "Get over to the Hendricks place if you can. They'll take care of you."

Inside the house, burning wood cracked with sounds like pistol shots. The barn, filled with grass hay, had caught more swiftly and now was like a giant torch. It lighted the yard and an area a hundred yards beyond with an orange glow that was almost as bright as day. In this light Sam could see their faces, and he knew if he lived he would never forget a single one of them. There was Shawcroft, grizzled and white-haired and as cold and hard of eye as a grizzly bear. There was the man who had roped him, skinny and bony and tall, grinning and showing yellowed teeth, but with the same mark of power and ruthlessness on him worn by the older man. There was the fat one, who looked scared, and the powerful-looking one with the Confederate cavalry officer's hat. The other three were plainly employees, identifiable not only by the way they were dressed but by the marks of toil that lay on them like a stain. They seemed reluctant, but they were plainly afraid to protest. They knew this was wrong but they hadn't the guts it took to say so, to take a stand for what they knew was right.

One of them finally did, though, as the wagon tongue raised to stand gaunt and menacing against the sky. "Mr. Shawcroft, hadn't we ought to let the man have his say?" he ventured.

The one with the cavalry officer's hat said, "What for? He'd only lie."

The fat one cleared his throat and said, "It wouldn't hurt."

Shawcroft said, "All right." He stared down at Sam. "Say what you got to say."

Sam gently released Prudence and got to his feet. He said, "A man don't lie when he's about to die. I didn't kill your beef. I didn't kill nobody's beef. But you'd better go ahead and kill me now that you've gone this far. Because if you don't I'm going to hunt down every last one of you."

Shawcroft's eyes were frosty. "That all you got to say?"

"My wife's hurt. She's five months along and she's been hurt. You see that she gets over to the Hendricks place."

The one that had dragged him laughed harshly. "Now he's tellin' us what to do."

Prudence was quiet now. He looked down at her. Each time a pain took her, it showed as a whitening around her mouth and tightening of her facial muscles. But she was biting her lip to avoid crying out. Blood ran from her lower lip and trickled down her chin.

It was her eyes that held his glance. She had accepted what was happening and she had faced, in her mind, what would happen now. She knew she had lost their child, or would, and she knew she was losing him. Furthermore, she knew there was nothing either of them could do.

The expression in her eyes was almost frightening. She stared first at Shawcroft's face, then at the thin one's face, then at the others, each in their turn. She was memorizing them, just as he had, only even more thoroughly.

Shawcroft said harshly, "He's had his say. Let's get on with it."

Sam Dunson knelt. "Good-bye, Prue."

She didn't seem to hear. There was only wildness in her eyes. He kissed her on the mouth and pushed himself to his feet. He asked, "Does she have to see?"

Shawcroft said, "Let her see. Maybe she'll tell some others."

Sam said, "You dirty, murderin' son-of-a-bitch!"

Shawcroft laughed bitterly, "It won't work, Dunson. You can't make me mad

15

enough to shoot you down. You're goin' to hang."

Dunson ran. It probably wouldn't do any good but he wasn't going to let himself meekly be hanged without putting up some kind of struggle. Maybe one of them, whose stomach wasn't as strong as those of the others, would shoot him down.

It was a forlorn hope. These were cattlemen. A rope sailed out, and he was yanked to a halt. He was dragged to the propped-up wagon tongue, from the end of which another rope dangled, a hangman's noose on its end.

His hands were tied behind his back and he was boosted onto a horse. The rope was harsh and rough around his already rope-burned neck.

They were mercifully swift. A rope end cracked against the horse's rump and the horse broke away. The yank broke Dunson's neck and killed him instantly. With his feet less than six inches from the ground, he swung back and forth, swaying the wagon tongue but not bringing it down. Prudence uttered one shrill scream as he was yanked from the back of the horse. She fainted, then, and lay still against the wall of the burning house.

Someone asked in a now-hushed voice,

"What do we do with her?"

Shawcroft said, "Drag her away from there so that she won't get burned."

"Ain't we going to take her to Hendricks'?"

Shawcroft said, "That woman's word ain't worth a damn against ours. But if Hendricks and his wife and son was to back her up, somebody might believe."

Two of the men lifted Prudence Dunson and carried her out away from the burning house. They laid her on the ground, then mounted and rode away.

Sam Dunson swung gently back and forth below the propped-up wagon tongue. In less than a minute, silence, except for the crackling of burning wood in house and barn, was absolute.

Prudence Dunson lay as if she too were dead.

Chapter 2

The pains woke her, bringing involuntary moans from her as they became too terrible to be borne. They were close together now, and she knew exactly what they meant. She was losing her child and, out here alone, there was nothing she could do to prevent it happening. Perhaps there would have been nothing that could have been done no matter where she was. The horse striking her had slammed her hard against the wall of the house. She had known, then, how great the danger of losing her baby was.

In the early hours preceding the dawn she gave birth to the unformed, premature thing that would eventually have become a child, and as soon as she could get up, she scratched a hole in the earth and buried it. The house was gone, only a smoldering pile of blackened rubble. So was the barn. Nothing was left but the empty corral, and the wagon, the tongue of which was raised and from which Sam still hung.

She had no knife, so laboriously and with great difficulty she sawed through the rope with a sharp piece of rock. She winced when it parted and he fell.

Never in her life had she imagined anything as terrible as this happening to her. Sam's face was hardly recognizable, so congested was it with blood. He was bare above the waist, dusty and crusted with dried blood. He was too heavy for her to lift, and she couldn't bury him because she had no shovel with which to dig. The hide of the steer he was supposed to have killed lay less than a dozen yards away from him.

The sun came up. She looked around, still numb from all that had happened to her. She had stood all that a human can and had somehow survived. Yet those faces were etched in her memory. Faces without bodies. Faces that hung suspended in space whenever she closed her eyes. Brutally and savagely and unjustly they had taken Sam from her. They had taken Sam's child from her belly, and they had destroyed what Sam had labored so long and hard to build. God might punish them, but she couldn't wait for that. There had to be a punishment for them on earth. She owed that much to Sam.

She was weak and exhausted from her ordeal, but there was something in her that would not let her rest. It drove her; it whipped her on. She headed toward the Hendricks place seven miles away. There was a narrow, two-track road that ran between their place and the Hendricks' because they had been good friends and had seen each other as often as time and work and distance would permit.

She had traveled less than half a mile when she stumbled and fell headlong. She tried to get up and failed. So she crawled until her hands and knees were raw.

Olaf Hendricks found her this way, having seen the faint plume of smoke rising from the rubble of house and barn when he got up and went out to milk the cow. He got off his horse and knelt beside her. He saw the blood on her, and the dust, and he saw the terrible look that was in her eyes.

Desperately he wanted to go on — to see what had happened at the Dunsons'. But Prue Dunson needed care, and now, so he lifted her to his saddle, and mounted behind her, turning his horse toward home.

When he arrived, he lifted her down, carried her into the house, and laid her on the bed. He let his wife take over, went out, and mounted his horse again. He suspected what he was going to find, so he took a shovel along with him. And a rifle. And his fifteen-year-old son.

What he found was what he had expected — Sam Dunson, lying on the ground dead, with the rope still around his neck. House and barn burned. Blood on the ground where Prudence had miscarried, and the freshly turned earth showing where she had buried what would eventually have been their child. Hendricks' son, Hector, had a grayish look about him as if he was going to be sick. Hendricks said, "Take the shovel and start a grave."

The boy took the shovel but did not immediately go to work. He asked, "Why, pa? Why? Mr. Dunson never hurt nobody."

Hendricks unrolled the soggy hide. He spread it out and read the brand. It was Shawcroft's Lazy S Quarter Circle.

He knew, then, what had happened, and why. He knew, too, that he would be next. They'd bring a green hide into his yard and accuse him of butchering it, and they'd hang him just as they had hanged Sam. It wouldn't matter that he hadn't butchered Shawcroft's steer. They'd try, convict, sentence, and execute him, all in ten or fifteen minutes, and that would be the end of it. They wanted the settlers gone from this part of Wyoming, and now that they'd hanged Sam the rest would come easy for them. All would know that anyone who stayed would die. They'd all been warned to leave and some already had. After this, it was doubtful if anyone would stay.

Hector said again, "Why'd they do it? Mr. Dunson never took nothing that didn't belong to him."

Hendricks said, "Dig, son. We'll bury him and get out of here. Maybe if we hurry we can still leave before dark."

"Leave? To go where, pa?"

"Anyplace. Anyplace where they don't murder you just for settling on the land."

Hector didn't say anything more. He walked away a little and began to dig.

There wasn't much Hendricks could do. Everything except Sam's rifle had been destroyed. He picked it up and tied it across the back of his saddle.

When Hector tired, he took over and dug until he himself was tired. Between them they finished the grave in an hour and a half. There was an urgency in Hendricks of which he wasn't very proud. But he knew he couldn't fight. Not the power of the cattlemen. Not when they were willing to resort to murder in the night to get the settlers off their range.

He couldn't lift Sam Dunson into the grave and he had no rope with which to lower him. So he rolled the body in, and it hit the bottom with a sodden thump. Hendricks wanted to pray over the grave, but there wasn't time for that either. He looked down and said, "God have mercy on you, Sam," and began to throw in the dirt, not looking because he was throwing dirt right into Sam Dunson's face. When the grave was filled and mounded over, he stuck the shovel in at the head of it, mounted his horse, and led away toward home. Hector followed, face pale, eyes downcast.

Coming into the yard, Hendricks rode straight to the corral. He caught the team and led them to the shed where the harness hung. He harnessed them, drove them to the wagon, and backed them into place. He hitched them up, then climbed to the seat, and drove the wagon to the house.

His wife came to the door. He said, "We'll make a bed for Mrs. Dunson in the back. We'll take everything we can — things that mean the most to us, and git. Sam Dunson was hanged last night because they said he butchered one of Shawcroft's steers."

Her eyes were stricken when he said they

were going to leave. Her face paled notice-
ably when he said Sam Dunson had been
hanged. But she didn't argue with him.
She knew they couldn't stay and fight.
This was her home but she valued the lives
of her family more than she did either
house or land or the things they would
have to leave. She knew as well as
Hendricks did that the night riders might
visit their place tonight.

They got out in the middle of the afternoon, the wagon piled high, Prudence
Dunson lying in the featherbed on top of the
load. Hector rode one of the saddlehorses
and drove the milk cow, her three-month-old
calf gamboling at her side. The other horse,
saddled, was tied behind the wagon.

They reached the town of Broken Arrow
at ten that night. Because they had little
money and would need all they had, they
camped in the willows at the edge of town.
Hendricks stretched a canvas tarp from the
wagon to two willow trees to shelter them
in case it rained.

Prudence Dunson left while they were
busy making camp. None of them saw her
go. They called and searched for half an
hour without result. Finally Hendricks
headed in to town, figuring that was where
she must have gone.

★ ★ ★

Prudence pretended to sleep all the way to town. She didn't want to talk. She didn't want them trying to cheer her up.

She still pretended sleep while they made camp, all the time watching for her chance. When they were all busy away from the wagon she climbed down out of it and hurried toward town.

She was stiff and bruised and sore, and her belly doubled her occasionally with cramps. It was agony to think so she didn't think. Pretty soon she saw some faint, winking lights ahead and shortly afterward came into town at the lower end of Shoshoni Street.

It was after ten and nearly everything was closed. All the stores were dark. There was a dim light in the lobby of the hotel, and on the second floor there was light coming from two of the windows that faced the street.

The sheriff's office and jail was a sand-stone block building that sat all by itself surrounded by weed-grown vacant lots. There was also a light in it.

Prudence went to it and knocked. She heard a cot creak inside and a few moments later the door opened.

She had only been to Broken Arrow

twice. But she knew the sheriff's face and she knew his name. "Sheriff Tate? I'm Prudence Dunson from out north of town."

He held the door for her. "Sure, Mrs. Dunson. I remember you. What can I do for you?"

She ought to be weeping, screaming hysterically at him that Sam was dead, murdered in the night for something he hadn't done. But here she was, talking politely and quietly as if nothing serious was on her mind. She said heavily, "Sam — my husband — is dead."

The sheriff was a stocky man, with a thick neck and a powerful body that seemed too heavy for the short, bowed legs that supported it. He said, "I'm sorry. Here, sit down. Sit down."

She sank into the chair. She knew he saw the blood on her clothes because he looked carefully at each spot of it. He said, "Maybe you'd better tell me all about it, ma'am."

She heard a voice that did not sound like her own. "They came in the night, seven of them. They accused him of butchering a steer and they dragged him out and murdered him."

"Shot him, you mean?"

"Hanged him. And when I got the rifle

to try and stop them, they slammed me against the side of the house. I . . . I lost my child."

The sheriff didn't seem to know what to say. Finally he managed, "Do you know who they were? Did you recognize any of them?"

She had the feeling that he knew without being told. She also had the feeling that nothing was going to come of it, even if she did name some of them. They would deny it, and their word would be accepted before that of a hysterical woman, and everybody would say they were sorry and would be glad when she got on the stage and left. Maybe they'd even take up a collection to pay her fare out of town.

She said, "Mr. Shawcroft was leading them. There was also a tall, very thin man, and a fat man, and one who wore a Confederate officer's campaign hat."

He said, "Are you sure? I can't believe that Mr. Shawcroft would. . . ."

She said, "He did. I heard him called by name."

The sheriff seemed to be at a loss for words. Prudence asked, "Aren't you going to do anything? Aren't you going to arrest my husband's murderers?"

He got up and walked to the window,

showing her his back. "Of course I am. If they done what you say they did. But, ma'am, it was dark. You was scared. How can you be sure?"

She got up too. She went to the door. Without speaking, she went out into the night.

He let her go without following, without protest. He knew it had happened just the way she said it had. He knew Shawcroft had been involved and he could put names to the others she had described.

The skinny one was Laughton, the fat one Gibbs, the one with the cavalry officer's campaign hat was Hardesty. The three with them had probably been employees.

But the sheriff also knew that nothing would ever be done to them. He could go out and question them but they'd deny everything. Furthermore, they would have been miles away from the Dunson place last night and there would be a reliable witness to swear to it. He could arrest them, but the county attorney would say there wasn't enough evidence to justify bringing them to trial.

He'd go through the motions, though, and then nobody could say he hadn't done his job. He put on his hat, shrugged into his sheepskin jacket, and headed for the livery stable to get his horse. He had a sour curse for the Wyoming Cattlemen's Association and its arrogant members as he walked along the darkened street.

Chapter 3

Sheriff Tate was not really surprised at the way they took his demand that they all surrender themselves in Broken Arrow at ten o'clock of the following day. They all had expected him; they all had their alibis; they all showed a willingness to cooperate with the law and expressed horror at the grisly murder of the night before. Tate returned to town, arriving at sunup, tired and irritable. He had given up a night's sleep and had accomplished nothing.

Hendricks was waiting for him when he reached the jail. Tate knew the man, knew he had been Sam Dunson's closest neighbor, and knew why he was here. He unlocked the door and invited Hendricks to come inside. He asked, "Is Mrs. Dunson staying with you?"

Hendricks nodded. "We're camped in the willows down by the creek."

"What can I do for you?"

"I want to know what you've done."

Tate stirred the ashes in his little pot-bellied stove, added some wadded-up newspapers and some sticks. He touched a match to it, closed the door, then put the coffee left over from last night on to heat. He said, "She named Mr. Shawcroft as their leader and she described three other men. I rode out to their ranches during the night and told them to show up at the courthouse at ten o'clock. If you will bring Mrs. Dunson there, she will have an opportunity to identify them."

Hendricks said, "And if she does?"

Tate shrugged, finding it difficult to meet Hendricks' glance. "Depends on what their story is, I guess. If they deny it, and if they can prove they were someplace else, why then I guess that's the end of it."

Hendricks clenched his fists. Muscles played along his jaw. He said, "You son-of-a-bitch, you're their bought-and-paid-for man."

Tate fought down the sudden surge of anger that came to him, because he knew it was caused not so much by Hendricks' words as by his own helplessness. He said, "I'm not their man. I do the best I can. But they're too powerful."

"What about the law? The law says we

31

got a right to homestead government land. The law says murder is a crime."

Tate asked wearily, "What do you want me to do? You tell me, and I'll do it."

"Arrest 'em. Charge them with what they done."

"Even if the judge would issue warrants, they'd be out on bail in an hour. The county attorney would tell me to let it drop." He poured himself a cup of thick black coffee, aware that his hand couldn't hold the cup steadily. Turning, he said, "I didn't make the world. I didn't make the rules. I just try to live with them, the same as everybody else. Maybe those four did kill Sam Dunson, but nobody can prove it and nobody ever will."

"And they'll get away with it?"

"Like I said, I didn't make the world." He was angry now because he was getting blamed for something that was not his fault.

Hendricks stamped out angrily. Tate gulped the scalding coffee and swore to himself that when his term was up he'd find something else to do. A long, long ways from here.

Hendricks and Prudence Dunson were at the courthouse at ten o'clock. The sheriff met them at the door and escorted them to the county courtroom. Four men were waiting inside. When Prudence saw them, she felt terror strike her like a blow. They were the same four who had hanged Sam night before last. One, the man with the Confederate cavalry officer's campaign hat, held now in his hands, was the one who had spurred his horse and knocked her against the house, causing the miscarriage of her child.

Awkward, it was, but Tate did the best he could. He said, "Mrs. Dunson, this is Mr. Shawcroft, and Mr. Laughton, Mr. Gibbs, and Mr. Hardesty." Gibbs was the fat one. His face was oily with sweat and his eyes had a strange, scared look to them. She did not acknowledge the introductions. All she said was, "They are the ones. Four of them, at least. There were three others."

Tate looked at the four. "What about it? I suppose you can prove where you were night before last?"

Shawcroft said, "I don't know about the others, sheriff, but I was in Cheyenne. Half a dozen people saw me there."

Tate looked at the others. "I suppose you've got alibis too."

Gibbs and Hardesty nodded. Laughton

33

said angrily, "I object to you calling them alibis."

Tate looked at Prudence Dunson. "You see, Mrs. Dunson?"

Her face was white and her eyes were furious. But she didn't say anything. She followed the sheriff out and thanked him perfunctorily on the courthouse steps. He asked, "What will you do now?"

She said, "Get a job. Do what you won't."

"What do you mean?"

"I mean that those men and the others who were with them are going to pay the lawful penalty for the murder of my husband and unborn child."

He looked at her long and hard. "Ma'am, don't try taking the law into your own hands. You're outclassed. You haven't got a chance against those men."

She did not bother to reply. He studied her, his expression changing subtly from one of sympathetic warning to one of puzzlement and alarm. Still shaking his head, he touched his hat brim and walked away.

Prudence stayed in front of the courthouse. Shawcroft and the other three came out. Shawcroft, Laughton, and Hardesty mounted their horses, which had been tied to the courthouse rail, and rode away, avoiding looking directly at her. Gibbs did look at her, then ducked his head and hurried up the street. Prudence followed him.

Gibbs went to a big three-story house sitting on a couple of acres of ground at the upper edge of town. He glanced back, saw her, then ducked in and slammed the door. Prudence stood across the street and watched the house.

The hours passed. Her legs ached and her belly burned like fire. But she remained standing there, almost motionless. Occasionally she saw the curtains stir in one window or another as Gibbs peered out. When she could no longer stand, she sat on the ground. She didn't take her eyes off the house.

When it was completely dark, when she could no longer be seen, she left. She returned to the Hendricks' camp in the willows at the edge of town. Both Hendricks and his wife were worried, but they had kept supper warm for her. She ate and went to her bed beneath the wagon. As soon as Hendricks and his wife were asleep, she got up, dressed, and put on her high-button shoes.

She took Sam's rifle, which Hendricks had picked up after he had buried Sam.

She checked to make sure it was loaded, and then, silently, she headed up through town again.

Keeping to the shadows, she made sure that she was not seen. She reached the Gibbs house, and circled it to the rear. There still were lights inside. Apparently cattle- men, even those living in town, did not retire as early as homesteaders did.

At the rear of the house, she waited. As she stood there, her eyes gradually became accustomed to the dark. She could see the stable behind the house, and beyond it an outhouse. Up near the back porch a barricade had been erected to keep anyone from falling into a well, in the process of being dug. Nearby was a huge pile of earth and several wagonloads of stone to be used for lining the well when the digging was done.

Prudence sat down on the ground. It would be easy to go away, to try starting life over again someplace else. In time she could probably learn to live with what had happened to Sam.

But the knowledge that his murderers were running around free, unpunished, would fester forever in her mind. How could she ever live with herself if she went away and let Sam and her unborn child go unavenged? Two lives had been taken wantonly. Until the killers paid for their act, she could never again know any peace.

One by one, the lights in the house went out. Except for a single lamp. It dimmed in an upstairs room as it was carried out and down the stairs. It came to the kitchen. It remained there as the back door opened.

Gibbs came out, clad in a white nightshirt. He headed for the outhouse in the dark.

Prudence intercepted him. He started violently when he saw her dim shape ahead of him. She said, "I want their names."

"Whose names? I don't know what you're talking about."

"You know. The names of the three who were with you when you hanged my husband night before last."

"See here, madam, you'd better leave!" he said shrilly. "I'll call the sheriff."

Prudence Dunson was scared and her teeth were chattering. Her hands were trembling so violently that the cocked and loaded rifle was in danger of going off accidentally. She jabbed it into Gibbs's fat belly as hard as she could, so hard it brought an involuntary grunt from him.

She had picked him because that morning at the courthouse he had showed how scared he was. She needed the other three names and she had figured Gibbs would be the most likely to cave in and give them to her. She said, "The names."

"And if I give them to you? What then?"

"I'll give you a better chance than you gave Sam. I'll let you make a run for it."

He hesitated only an instant more. He was shivering even more violently than Prudence was, partly perhaps from the chill of the night, but mostly from the terror of having a gun jabbed into his belly. He said, "All right, all right. One was Montoya, the Mexican that works out at Shawcroft's place."

He stopped. He didn't want to give his own man away, but the pressure of the gun muzzle was inexorable. He said, "My foreman Finney was there."

"And who was the third?"

"McAndrews. He works for Hardesty."

The names were etched as plainly in Prudence Dunson's memory as the seven faces were. She said, "All right. I said you could run for it. But you'd better travel fast because I'm going to kill you if I can." She almost managed to keep the tremor out of her voice. Almost, not quite.

Gibbs broke away. She raised the gun and fired. The sound was shocking in the utter stillness of the night.

Gibbs, heading straight for the back door and the light, veered at the sound of the shot. Blindly he crashed through the barricade that surrounded the fresh-dug well.

He screamed as he fell in, his scream diminishing as he tumbled to the bottom of the well. Then all was silent, except for a plaintive call from an upstairs window, "Henry? Whatever are you doing? Was that a gunshot I heard?"

Prudence hurried into the alley and along it to the street. A few lights in houses near the Gibbs place went on. She hurried through town, taking care to stay in the shadows, and eventually reached the willows where the Hendricks' wagon was.

Silently and unnoticed, she crept to her bed underneath the wagon and pulled the blanket over her.

She hadn't killed Gibbs but she had caused his death. And now she knew something she hadn't known before. She could go on with it. She could kill if it was necessary. Her husband and her child would be avenged.

Why, then, did she begin to weep? Why were the sobs torn from deep inside her so forcefully that she could not conceal their sound even though she buried her face in her wadded-up blanket.

Hendricks and his wife awoke, and heard, and thought they understood. But they did not understand. Even Prudence Dunson did not wholly understand.

Chapter 4

At seven o'clock, Sheriff Jason Tate went to the livery stable and got his horse. He mounted, rode down the hollow-sounding plank incline to the street, and headed toward the Hendricks' camp at the edge of town.

He had been up a good part of the night, supervising the recovery of Gibbs's body from the partially dug well, trying to calm Mrs. Gibbs afterward. She had bitterly accused Prudence Dunson, saying Prudence had stood across the street most of the day watching their house. She had mentioned her husband's nervousness, his apparent fear. And she had told him about the single gunshot in the back yard last night just after her husband had headed for the outhouse before retiring.

He had not come back. Fearful for his safety, she had searched the yard, but without results. Then she had gone after

Sheriff Tate. Tate had found the broken barricade. A lantern lowered into the well had revealed Gibbs's crumpled, motionless body.

There was already a fire at the Hendricks' camp. Mrs. Hendricks and Prudence were preparing breakfast. The Hendricks' boy, Hector, was a couple of hundred yards downstream gathering firewood. Hendricks himself was greasing one of the wagon wheels.

Tate thought Prudence had trouble meeting his glance. He sat on his horse, patiently waiting for an invitation to dismount. It didn't come. Both Mrs. Hendricks and her husband stared coldly up at him.

He couldn't blame them for their hostility. They had expected justice in the murder of Sam Dunson and he hadn't provided it. He took off his hat and rested it on the saddle horn in front of him. He said, "Good morning, folks."

Nobody answered him. He studied Prudence Dunson openly. Under his steady scrutiny, her face flushed. After that first glance up at him, she kept her eyes downcast.

She was a pretty woman, not yet made stringy and leather-skinned by the hardships of this land. Her hair was dark brown, shining in the sun. Her eyes were warm despite their color, which was gray. Her mouth was full and soft when it was not compressed. Tate said, "I have to ask you some questions, Mrs. Dunson."

Hendricks growled, "The ones you ought to be askin' questions of is them damn murderin' cowmen!"

Tate ignored him. He asked bluntly, "Did you kill Henry Gibbs, Mrs. Dunson?"

She started visibly. She did not immediately look up but she showed no surprise.

Hendricks said, "Gibbs? Is he dead? Good riddance, if you ask me."

Tate tried again. "Mrs. Dunson?"

She finally raised her glance. He thought there was pain in her eyes, but he could not be sure that was what he saw. He repeated, "Did you kill Henry Gibbs, Mrs. Dunson?"

She looked him straight in the eye. "No sir, I did not."

Hendricks snorted, " 'Course she didn't! How could she? She was asleep right here all night. How did Gibbs die, anyway?"

"Fell down his well. His wife said there was a shot fired just before he disappeared."

"Find the bullet wound?"

Tate shook his head helplessly. He was sure in his own mind that Prudence Dunson was responsible, but he didn't know how she had managed it, and he knew he'd never prove anything even if he wanted to. He also knew he had a job to do.

Hendricks said, "Then get out of here an' stop houndin' this poor woman. Ain't it enough . . . well, about the way her husband died an' everything?"

Tate felt his face growing hot with embarrassment. He said, "It's not quite that simple, I'm afraid. Mrs. Gibbs has signed a complaint. I'm going to ask you to come with me, Mrs. Dunson."

Hendricks stared up incredulously, wiping his greasy hands on an equally greasy rag. "You serious? You actually going to throw her into jail?"

Tate wondered why the hell he had picked this line of work. He couldn't look at Hendricks or at his wife. He said helplessly, "I'm sorry, but I haven't got any choice."

Hendricks exploded, "Well I'll be damned! You won't arrest a bunch of murderin' cowmen, but you'll come down here and arrest a helpless woman. By God, Tate, you're really somethin'!"

44

Tate knew his face was a dull, brick red. He wished he was anyplace but here. Oddly, it was Prudence Dunson who tried to make him feel better about what he had to do. She said softly, "All right, Mr. Tate. I'll come with you."

Hendricks asked sarcastically, "You going to handcuff her, sheriff? She's mighty dangerous."

Prudence Dunson said, "I'm ready, sheriff."

"You can finish your breakfast, ma'am. There isn't all that much rush."

"No, Sheriff Tate. I guess I am not very hungry." She walked toward him.

He dismounted. He walked beside her back toward town. Behind him, he could hear Hendricks grumbling and cursing, could hear Mrs. Hendricks chiding him for the profanity. The Hendricks' boy had brought in a load of firewood and now stood staring after the departing pair.

Prudence Dunson said, "Don't feel badly, Mr. Tate. I understand that this is something you have to do."

Helplessly Tate said, "She signed a complaint, ma'am. I didn't have any choice." It struck him even as he said it that he had said it before, recently. It also struck him that, in matters involving conflicts between the big ranchers and those who were in their way, he seldom had any choice. They manipulated events and people so that they always came out on top.

But they would have a hell of a time proving that Prudence Dunson had caused the death of Henry Gibbs. Hendricks and his wife would swear she was at their camp that night. There was no bullet wound on Henry Gibbs. No matter how Mrs. Gibbs or the cowmen tried, they could never convince anyone that Prudence Dunson had thrown Gibbs down the well.

The pair walked in awkward silence for a while. Finally Tate asked, "Do you know yet what you're going to do, Mrs. Dunson?"

"That will have to wait on the outcome of this arrest, won't it, Sheriff Tate?"

He said, "There's not much doubt about how this is going to come out. I don't think it likely anyone is going to prove you threw Gibbs down his well."

She did not reply. They walked the rest of the way to the jail in silence, Tate's temper growing with every step he took. He felt strong sympathy for Mrs. Dunson, anger at the powerful cowmen for what they had done to her. He wished there was some way he could make things right but he couldn't see what it would be. They reached the jail and he held the door for her. She glanced around the office in dismay, then looked toward the cells at the rear. She started toward them but Tate said quickly, "No need for that, Mrs. Dunson."

"Aren't you going to lock me up?"

"No ma'am."

"Then what are you going to do with me?"

He tipped back his hat and scratched his head. "I don't know."

She couldn't help smiling at his puzzlement. He stared past her and out the window. People were gathering across the street. He saw the Hendricks family and three other families of displaced settlers who had camped near Hendricks at the edge of town. A number of townspeople had joined the settlers. There must be nearly thirty people gathered watching the jail, he thought. They didn't look dangerous but they were obviously angry, and Tate knew both their anger and their numbers would grow if he held Prudence Dunson in jail for any length of time. He said, "Ma'am, I'm going to ask you to do something that might sound peculiar to you."

"What is that, Mr. Tate?"

He noticed that she had started calling him Mr. Tate instead of Sheriff Tate. He liked the change. He said, "I'm going to ask you to stay here while I go talk to Mrs. Gibbs. If I can get her to withdraw that complaint it will save a lot of trouble all around."

"All right, Mr. Tate. I'll stay until you come back."

"Will you lock the door and not let anybody inside?"

"Yes, if you want me to."

"I do." He went to the door and stepped outside, closing it behind him. He heard the bolt shoot home.

Hendricks yelled at him, "You got her locked in tight, sheriff?"

He glanced toward the crowd. There was a growing, angry murmur over there. He did not reply, but turned and walked toward the Gibbs house. A couple of taunts were yelled at him but he didn't pause or turn.

Jacob Henshaw, the Methodist preacher, was at Mrs. Gibbs's house, along with his wife. All three were sitting in the darkened parlor having tea. Mrs. Gibbs's eyes were red from weeping and her face was pale.

Tate stepped inside, removing his hat as he did. Henshaw said, "We'll be going,

Mrs. Gibbs."

Tate said, "No need. I'm not going to be here long and I've nothing to say that you can't hear."

Mrs. Gibbs said, "Please stay. It's such a comfort having you and I hate to be alone."

Henshaw sank back into his chair. Tate said, "Mrs. Gibbs, I can't see any way that Mrs. Dunson could have been responsible for Henry's death. He was a pretty good-sized man and she's not very big."

"She could have shot at him. She could have scared him enough to make him run. It could be that he was trying to get away from her when he went down the well." She began to cry again and dabbed at her eyes with a lacy handkerchief.

Tate said, "The Hendricks family says she was out at their camp all night. They say she was asleep."

"She could've got up. They wasn't awake all night, was they?"

"I don't suppose they were."

"Besides that, who else could it be?"

He could have given her a dozen names but this was neither the time nor place. He said, "I wish you'd withdraw that complaint, Mrs. Gibbs. People are getting all stirred up."

"What people?"

"Settlers that your husband, Shawcroft, Laughton, and Hardesty have forced off their land. Townspeople who are in sympathy with them."

"My husband denied doing that. So did Mr. Shawcroft and Mr. Laughton and Mr. Hardesty."

"I know they denied it, ma'am. But I know they did it and I think you do too. The four of them burned Mrs. Dunson's home. They hanged her husband and caused her to lose her child. They've got away with it so far because they all had people willing to swear they were a long ways from there when it happened, but they went too far, hanging Sam Dunson the way they did."

Mrs. Gibbs wept quietly into her handkerchief. When she finally looked up, she directed her glance toward the Reverend Henshaw. "What would you say I should do?"

Henshaw said, "There is no proof. She will be acquitted even if she goes to trial."

There were no tears now in Mrs. Gibbs's eyes. Her mouth was a straight and angry line. "I hate to think she is going to get away with it."

Tate wanted to say he hated to think of

the four cattlemen getting away with Sam Dunson's murder, but he had the good sense to keep the thought to himself.

Mrs. Gibbs said, "All right. I withdraw the complaint."

Tate nodded. "Thank you, Mrs. Gibbs." He ducked out the door before she had a chance to change her mind. He hurried back to the jail.

The crowd in front of it had grown. He knocked on the door, and when Prudence Dunson asked who it was, he told her and she unlocked the door. He went in. "It's all right. She's agreed to drop the complaint. The preacher was there and he kind of helped me talk her into it."

"Then I'm free to go?"

"Yes ma'am. And I'm sorry I had to bring you here."

"Thank you for getting her to withdraw the complaint."

He nodded, glad it was over, glad he wasn't going to have to worry about that crowd. He opened the door for Prudence Dunson and watched her step out into the street.

Hendricks and his wife and son hurried across to her. Tate withdrew into the jail and closed the door.

He was sure in his own mind that Prudence Dunson had fired the shot in Henry Gibbs's backyard last night. He was reasonably sure the shot had frightened Gibbs enough to make him run blind through the barricade around the well.

But he couldn't blame Prudence for doing what she had done. Gibbs had been a killer the law could not touch.

What worried him was the effect all this would have on Prudence Dunson herself. Murder wasn't something decent people could get involved in and remain unchanged. If she went on, and he suspected that she would, she would be changed from the person she now was into a sour, bitter woman, tormented by guilt and remorse. Her revenge would cost her, if not her freedom or her life, at least her chance for happiness and peace of mind.

He also suspected that nothing he could say to her would lessen her determination to avenge her husband's death.

Chapter 5

There were conflicting emotions in Prudence as she walked across the street toward the Hendricks family and the others. She would not have been human if she had not been pleased by their support, even though she knew it was, in reality, support for justice as much as support for her personally.

What would they think, she wondered, if they knew she was really guilty of the death of Henry Gibbs? Would they continue their support? She doubted it.

However she might try to justify herself, the fact remained that she had caused the death of another human being. She was no better than Shawcroft, Hardesty, Laughton and Gibbs. She had no more right to take human life than they. She might ease her conscience by telling herself she was only doing what the law could not, or even by trying to convince herself she was acting as an instrument of the Almighty, but she was too honest for such self-deception. She was guilty of killing Gibbs, even if she hadn't laid a hand on him. She would have to admit it, take the blame, and try to live with it as best she could.

Gibbs had helped hang Sam, she reminded herself desperately. He had helped cause the death of her unborn child. He had helped burn her house and drive her away from her home. Gibbs had deserved to die and so did the other six.

There was suddenly a babble of voices around her, friendly, congratulatory voices that yanked her out of her preoccupation and back to reality. These were simple, decent people, glad that she had been released from jail, glad she would not be persecuted further. She smiled at them, and spoke, and then walked along with Hendricks and his wife and son. Settlers, camped near the Hendricks family, walked with them. Others, the townspeople, left the group and went back to their daily tasks.

Prudence had, by sheer determination, put aside her uneasy feelings of guilt over Gibbs's death. Now she was thinking grimly of Laughton, and Hardesty, and Shawcroft, and of those three others who had worked for them and who had helped hang Sam.

She knew that if she was going to stay here and avenge Sam, she would need some kind of job. She would need a place to stay and a means to support herself.

She waited until they reached the Hendricks' camp. She waited until the other settlers had dispersed. Then she told Hendricks and his wife, "I'm going back to town. I have to find a job."

"You don't need a job. You can stay with us until we leave and then you can come along."

Prudence shook her head. "I am staying. Sam is buried here. We have land and I do not intend to give it up."

Their protests died when they saw the determination in her face. She said goodbye, turned, and headed back toward town. Hendricks and his wife looked after her as if they did not understand at all.

She walked quickly. She had never held a job in her entire life. She wasn't qualified for very many jobs, but she could clean, wash and iron, cook and sew. She would, therefore, have to find a job doing one or more of those things she knew.

She supposed the hotel would be a good place to start. She headed up Shoshoni Street toward it — a tall, yellow building with a wide veranda along the two sides of it that faced the street, and elaborate scrollwork around the eaves and second-story balconies.

Several men sitting on the veranda stared at her as she climbed the steps, crossed the hollow-sounding floor, and went in through the double lobby doors. Inside, it was cool, dark by comparison with the sun glare outside. The floor was of white tile, the furniture heavy, dark, and upholstered with leather. A huge, shaggy buffalo head adorned the wall behind the desk. Bright Indian rugs were scattered at random on the lobby floor.

A woman was behind the desk, a stocky, middle-aged woman with a lined and leathery face. Prudence said, "I'm Prudence Dunson. I'm looking for a job."

The woman's blue eyes seemed to look straight through her. The voice that came from the woman's wide mouth was as rough and as harsh as the rest of her.

"I know who you are. What kind of job do you want?"

"Any kind. Any kind that will permit me to stay."

"You know what Shawcroft and them others are goin' to think if I give you a job?"

Prudence smiled faintly. "I can imagine."

The woman studied her. "I heard about Henry Gibbs. Heard about you bein' arrested, too."

Prudence waited. She couldn't tell from this woman's tough, leathery face what she was thinking.

The woman came from behind the desk. She stuck out her hand and Prudence took it. It was like shaking hands with a man. The woman said, "I'm Anne Jellico. My husband and me started this hotel thirty years ago when there wasn't nothing here but a corral and store."

Anne Jellico studied her, some approval now showing in her eyes. "You don't look it, but you got to have a lot of sand in your craw. Sure, I'll give you a job and to hell with them cowmen. Time somebody spit in their eye. Time somebody told 'em they wasn't God just because they got more cows than they can count. Come on, I'll fix you up with a room." She dug into a pocket of the loose-hanging sweater she was wearing and brought out a worn leather pocketbook. She opened it and withdrew two twenty-dollar gold pieces. She gave them to Prudence. "Here's your first month's pay. Way they burnt you out an' all, I don't figure you got much more'n the clothes on your back."

Prudence felt a lump forming in her throat at the unexpected kindness she was being shown. She said, "Thank you. I. . . ."

"Never mind that. You'll earn your pay. Come on now and I'll show you your room."

Prudence followed her to the stairs. Anne Jellico climbed them heavily, favoring her right leg and limping for several steps after they reached the top. She stopped at the door of a room at the end of the hall, took a key from her pocket, and unlocked the door. She went inside.

Prudence followed her. It was a bleak room but it was better than nothing. She said, "I'm ready to start work right away."

"Wait until morning. Get yourself settled first."

"Thank you." Prudence knew, if Anne Jellico did not, that Shawcroft and the others would put pressure on her to get rid of her new employee. She didn't know whether Anne Jellico could be pressured or whether she could not. She'd find out in the next day or two, she supposed.

Anne left and Prudence went out soon afterward. She headed for the store to buy a change of clothes so that she could wash and iron the ones she had on. She would need a few other things, but she meant to spend the forty dollars as sparingly as she could.

In early afternoon, Billy Williams, who worked at the bank, came into the hotel. He hurried across the lobby to the desk and looked at Anne Jellico. He said, "Howdy, Mrs. Jellico. Mr. Coulter sent me to ask if you'd come down to the bank."

"What for? Did he say?"

"No ma'am."

"All right. Tell him I'll be there in ten or fifteen minutes."

"Yes ma'am." Billy hurried out, gangling and young, with yellow hair curling over his ears.

Anne Jellico thought she knew what the summons was about, but she waited deliberately for twenty minutes before she headed for the bank.

It stood on the next corner down Shoshoni Street, built of gray sandstone, with bars at the windows and an ironwork grille that could be padlocked to protect the front door at night. A sign over the door read *Cattlemen's Bank & Trust, Est. 1869.* Anne Jellico opened the door and stepped inside.

The floor, like that of the hotel lobby, was of white tile. There was a shiny brass cuspidor beside each of the two brass-grilled teller windows. Anne went through the gate and headed for Jake Coulter's office in the rear.

Coulter got to his feet as she came in. He was a balding, middle-aged man, with a prominent paunch and a round, jowled face. Bright blue eyes peered at her from beneath very bushy brows. She said, "You ain't sent for me once in all these years. What's this all about?"

He looked flushed, a little embarrassed, and angry because he wasn't fooling anyone. He said, "I didn't tell you when it happened because I didn't see any need. But about a year ago, Norman Shawcroft bought your note from the bank."

Anne Jellico stared at him. "You mean you can sell a person's note without even asking them?"

"Of course. It's standard practice. There's nothing wrong with it."

"Except I end up owin' money to a man I wouldn't borrow from if he was the last damn man on earth."

Coulter said, "I'm sorry. But there was nothing wrong with it. Banks do it every day."

"All right," she said wearily. "What does he want?"

60

Coulter looked more embarrassed than before. "You've hired that Dunson woman to work at the hotel."

Anne Jellico nodded. "I thought that was it. He wants me to get rid of her. Ain't that it?"

Coulter nodded sheepishly.

"Or what?"

"He won't renew your note."

"Well to hell with him. When it comes due, you loan me the money to pay it off."

Coulter stared at her miserably. "I'm afraid I can't do that."

"What do you mean, you can't do that? You've held a note on the hotel for years. Ever since we put the second story on."

"I can't do it, Anne. I'm sorry."

"You're sorry? What the hell good does that do me? That son-of-a-bitch Shawcroft will just come in and take my hotel!"

"He don't want your hotel. All he wants is for you to get rid of that woman."

"And what if I do? What's he going to want me to do next?"

"Nothing. He's authorized me to execute a new twenty-year note. At a lower rate of interest than on the existing one, I might add."

Anne Jellico stared at Coulter in disgust. She knew when she was beat. She nodded

61

sourly. "All right. I guess Shawcroft wins. Make the goddamn new note. I'll go back to the hotel and fire her."

Angrily, she stormed out of the bank. As soon as she could, she meant to get the money someplace else and pay Shawcroft off. In the meantime she had no choice but to do what he demanded of her.

She consoled herself with the thought that maybe it was better all around. If Prudence Dunson stayed, she was going to try getting even with all the cattlemen who had killed her husband and burned her home. Better for her if she gave the idea up and went back East.

But she was not convinced.

Chapter 6

Prudence returned to the hotel in mid-afternoon, her arms loaded with packages. She went straight to her room and dumped them on the bed. She started to remove her clothes to try the new ones on, and stopped when there was a knock upon her door.

She opened it to find Anne Jellico standing in the hall. She said, "Come in, Mrs. Jellico."

Anne Jellico came into the room. Prudence noticed the expression on her face and knew instantly that something was wrong. She waited, not unwrapping any of the packages. A sinking feeling in her stomach told her what Anne Jellico had come to say.

Anne said harshly, without preamble, "I got to let you go."

Prudence felt the shock of it but without any real surprise. "The cattlemen?"

"Uh-huh. I borrowed five thousand dollars years ago to put the second story on the hotel. Seems like Shawcroft's come in and bought my note from the bank. It's up for renewal in three months and he says he won't renew unless I get rid of you."

Prudence Dunson's feelings were mixed. She didn't want to lose this job because having it meant she could stay and pursue her quest for revenge. Still, she knew that the pressure Shawcroft had put on Anne Jellico meant that he was scared. Scared of a lone, helpless woman. The realization gave her a heady feeling of triumph. With sudden dismay she said, "I have already spent some of the money." She started gathering packages from the bed. "Perhaps I can return these and get the money back."

Angrily Anne Jellico said, "They didn't say I had to get the forty dollars back. Least I can do is insist that you keep it."

"It wouldn't be right. I haven't earned it." Prudence began rummaging in the pocketbook she had bought.

Almost explosively, Anne Jellico said, "No! Damn it, I ain't going to take the money back! And I ain't going to throw you out of the hotel! You can stay here until you get something else."

The woman's voice was so emphatic that its sincerity could not be questioned. Prudence said, "All right. But I will repay you when I can."

"If it makes you feel better." Anne Jellico stared miserably at her. "I'm sorry. I'm just damn sorry."

"It's all right."

"What are you going to do now?"

Prudence felt a sudden helplessness. She didn't know what she was going to do. She had no money but what was left of the forty dollars. She couldn't stay at the hotel very long or she'd get Anne Jellico into more trouble over her note. She shook her head. "I don't know."

Anne Jellico hesitated and finally she said, "Shawcroft wouldn't of bothered to put pressure on me if he wasn't scared."

Prudence nodded numbly. Anne stared at her a moment more, then hastily left the room.

Prudence went to the window and stood there looking down into the street. She could feel scalding tears threatening to flood her eyes. She clenched her fists and thought of Sam. She remembered his words, "They're going to kill me, Prue." She thought of the way his last thoughts had been for her. "Get to the Hendricks if you can. They'll take care of you." She remembered cutting him down and the way his face had looked, bloated and congested with blood until he didn't even look like himself anymore. She remembered her own agony, bringing forth her unformed, premature child. The flood of tears receded before her returning anger and thirst for revenge. Right now she didn't know what she was going to do. But she knew she was not going to give up.

Keep busy, she thought. Keep busy and an idea will come. She changed clothes quickly, wrapped her soiled ones, and with the bundle beneath her arm, hurried out into the street. She walked quickly toward the edge of town where the Hendricks family was camped.

She spent the afternoon washing and ironing her clothes, and when she had finished wrapped them carefully again. She had supper with the Hendricks and after that walked back to the hotel. From Anne Jellico she got directions for reaching the Laughton ranch. Tomorrow, she thought, she would hire a buggy and drive out there. What she would do when she arrived, she had no idea, but maybe an idea would come to her.

She slept fitfully, awakening often. Her dreams were tormented. She relived the cattlemen's hanging of Sam and the burning of their home. She relived the death of Henry Gibbs and awoke, hearing his diminishing yell as he fell to the bottom of the well. She was bathed with perspiration and yet she was very cold.

At dawn she arose. She had coffee and oatmeal in the hotel dining room, trying not to pay attention to the curious stares of others eating breakfast there. When she was finished, she went out and hurried to the livery stable.

A horse and buggy was a dollar and a half for the day. She climbed in, slapped the horse's back with the reins, and drove out into the street. She took the road to the Laughton ranch.

She had selected Laughton's ranch for her visit because it was the closest of the three to town. Both Shawcroft and Hardesty lived farther away by at least a dozen miles.

She had no idea what she would do when she arrived. She tried to make her mind blank as she drove, but it was not easy. Memories of Sam came back, of strong, stocky, gentle Sam. She suddenly missed him terribly, and against her will her eyes filled once more with tears.

Angrily she clenched her fists. Crying wasn't going to accomplish anything except to make her weak.

Laughton's gate was so far from the buildings that they looked like toys in the distance. She got out of the buggy, opened the gate, led the horse through, and closed it behind her. She got into the buggy again and drove toward the distant cluster of buildings.

The house was huge, a brown-shingled, three-story building with gables over all of the third-story windows. Beyond was a big red barn and a number of other buildings. Chickens scratched in the bare area between house and barn. A few pigs slept in the shade of the barn and a couple of others rooted in some mud near the watering trough just inside the corral. Prudence clipped the tether weight to the horse's bridle and approached the back porch.

She had no idea what her reception was going to be. She had no idea what she was going to say. What if Laughton himself answered the door? She was scared, but anger and outrage suddenly drowned her fear. This man, Laughton, was one of those who had come riding into her yard at night. He was the skinny one. She knocked on the door, and when she got no immediate result, banged harder with her fist.

A woman came from the kitchen door

and crossed the porch, a look of surprise and puzzlement on her face. "Yes?"

She was a tall, gaunt woman with skin like leather and gray hair done up in a bun on her neck. Maybe Laughton was wealthy and maybe he had thousands of cattle, but this woman looked like any farm woman used to doing for herself and working hard. Prudence said, "I'm Prudence Dunson. I'm looking for Mrs. Laughton."

"I'm Mrs. Laughton." There was still puzzlement in the woman's eyes. "Won't you come in?"

"I don't want to come in."

"Then what do you want?"

"I want to tell you what your husband has done."

A strange look now came to Mrs. Laughton's face, one of resignation and disillusionment. "What has he done?"

"Hanged my husband. Caused me to lose my child. Burned our home."

"Oh, my God!" The exclamation seemed wrenched from Mrs. Laughton's mouth. She came outside. She seemed to want to put her arms around Prudence, but she didn't. She said, "When?"

"Several nights ago."

"Just him? Or were others with him?"

"Six others," Prudence said dully. "Mr.

69

Shawcroft, Mr. Hardesty, Mr. Gibbs, and three men who worked for them."

Now Mrs. Laughton's voice was bitter. "And they claimed later to have been fifty miles away. And there were witnesses who would swear they were. And the sheriff told you he was helpless to do anything."

"Yes. How did you know?"

"Because the same sort of thing has happened before." Mrs. Laughton was eyeing the rifle in Prudence's hand. "What are you going to do?"

"Kill him. If the law won't do it, I will."

"He isn't here."

"I'll wait."

"If you kill him, you will go to jail. The others will get away."

That statement confused Prudence. Mrs. Laughton said softly, "I will have to testify against you. I will have no choice."

Prudence felt tears of frustration threatening to flood her eyes. Mrs. Laughton said, "There has to be another way."

Prudence stared at her unbelievingly. "You are just trying to save him! You are trying to talk me out of killing him!" Her control was slipping and her voice was almost a scream.

"I am trying to save you, child. He is not worth saving. I have put up with his playing God for twenty years. He has hanged rustlers and horse thieves. He has killed anyone who got in his way. And for what? For more cattle. For more land. For more money in the bank." Her mouth firmed suddenly. "I won't be a part of it anymore. I'm going to leave. Would you let me ride back to town with you?"

Prudence stared at her with blurred eyes. The gaunt, weathered face was lined by years. She couldn't doubt the expression in Mrs. Laughton's eyes. She nodded numbly, knowing that Mrs. Laughton was right. Killing Laughton in cold blood would only get her sent to prison, and the other five men would escape her vengeance.

Mrs. Laughton took a battered black straw hat from a nail beside the door. She put it on and walked with Prudence to the buggy. A man stared curiously toward the buggy from the barn. Mrs. Laughton called, "I'm going to town. Tell Mr. Laughton I will not be back." She picked up the tether weight and unclipped it. She put it on the floor of the buggy before climbing in.

Prudence drove out of the yard and up the long road toward the gate. Once, looking back, she saw the man Mrs. Laughton had spoken to mounting a horse.

He rode out of the yard at a gallop, raising a dust cloud behind. Mrs. Laughton's face was grim. "He is going to tell my husband that I have gone."

"Will he come after us?"

"Yes. He'll come after us."

Prudence shifted the rifle so that she held it between her knees. Mrs. Laughton said, "You will not need that. He will not harm you. He does not make war on women."

Prudence asked bitterly, "Doesn't he?"

Mrs. Laughton did not reply. Prudence slapped the buggy horse's back with the reins and the animal broke into a trot. At the gate, Mrs. Laughton climbed down and opened it. Prudence drove through. Mrs. Laughton closed it and climbed back into the buggy with her.

Again Prudence slapped the buggy horse's back with the reins, forcing him to trot. A feeling of urgency possessed her and a strange feeling of dread. She did not want Laughton overtaking them. She did not want to be part of a confrontation between him and his wife.

Her own inconsistency confused her. She ought to welcome the chance to see him humiliated, to see him suffer, to see him angered at his own helplessness.

She took the buggy whip out of its socket and flayed the horse's back, making him break into a lope. The buggy careened from side to side, raising a towering cloud of dust.

Mrs. Laughton watched Prudence's face, paying little or no attention to the way the buggy was rocking from side to side. Prudence fought desperately for control, angry at herself for her weakness, for the way tears came every time she became confused or afraid.

She made herself think of Sam, who had always been calm and strong, and she felt a measure of her own calmness coming back.

She couldn't have said how she knew it, but she knew Laughton would overtake the buggy before it got to town. She gripped the rifle tighter between her knees and put all her attention on keeping the buggy upright and in the road.

Chapter 7

They were still a couple of miles from town
when Prudence heard, over the sounds of
the buggy horse's hoofs and the creaking of
the rig itself, the pounding of a horse's hoofs
behind. She turned her head and saw
Laughton overtaking them, his horse at a
run.

Mrs. Laughton said, "You might as well
stop."

Prudence drew the buggy horse to a halt.
Dust, raised by the buggy wheels and by
Laughton's running horse, rolled over the
buggy and settled on the two women.

Laughton yanked his plunging horse to a
halt beside the buggy on Mrs. Laughton's
side. He was as gaunt as she was, as weathered, too. There was a two- or three-day
growth of graying whiskers on his face. His
eyes, blue as ice, were angry and hard.
"What the hell do you think you're doing?"
he shouted.

Prudence's hands were knuckle-white against the rifle stock, but she made no move to raise and bring it to bear. She knew if she did, Laughton would draw the revolver he wore in a holster at his side, and while she didn't know if he'd shoot her or not, she briefly thought that it would be one way of getting rid of her. Let him shoot her, then let him try to escape the consequences. The trouble with that solution was that she'd be dead and Shawcroft and Hardesty and the other three would get away with what they had done.

Mrs. Laughton said, "I am leaving you, James. I am doing what I should have done many years ago."

Laughton's face turned brick-red with rage. "Like hell you are! You get out of that goddamn rig and get up on this horse with me!"

"No." Mrs. Laughton's voice was low-pitched, betraying her tension and her fear, but it was calm and sure. She turned her head. "Drive on, Mrs. Dunson."

"Dunson?" said Laughton. "I thought I recognized her, by God! What kind of damn lies has she been telling you?"

"Not lies. Truth. You forget how well I know you, James. You forget the rustlers and the horse thieves and some that were neither that you simply wanted to be rid of."

"I wasn't there," he roared. "I was. . . ."

His wife interrupted him. "You were there. You hanged Mrs. Dunson's husband. You burned her home. You caused her to lose her child." Her voice was dull, almost lifeless, like that of a judge pronouncing sentence.

"That's a lie! Hardesty. . . ." He stopped.

"Hardesty did what?"

In a voice that seemed scarcely audible, Prudence said, "Hardesty was the one who slammed me against the house and caused me to lose my child."

Mrs. Laughton stared at her husband with angry scorn. "And you think that because Hardesty was the one who did that you are free of responsibility?"

"I wasn't even there. I told you that before." His voice was sullen now.

Mrs. Laughton turned her head toward Prudence again. "Drive on, Mrs. Dunson. I have nothing more to say to him."

Prudence lifted her hands preparatory to slapping the buggy horse's back with the reins. That was as far as she got. Laughton bawled, "No, by God! You ain't leavin' *me*." He spurred his horse and forced the plunging, frightened animal toward the

76

buggy. The horse's chest came up hard against it, rocking it, threatening to overturn it. Before that could happen, Laughton reached down and seized his wife. He dragged her out bodily, but as she cleared the buggy, the material of her dress, which he had seized, tore loose and let her fall helplessly into the dust.

The buggy horse tried to bolt, but Prudence hauled back on the reins with all her strength. Unable to run, the horse reared, forcing the buggy backward ten or fifteen feet as he danced back on his two hind legs.

Laughton stepped from his own plunging, frightened horse. He approached his wife, who was struggling to get to her feet. Reaching down, he seized her by an arm and dragged her up. She tried to break free, and now thoroughly enraged and out of his head, he struck her with his fist.

She slumped and collapsed in a heap at his feet in the dusty road. He stooped to seize her again. Prudence screamed, "Stop! Stop or I'll shoot!" She had raised the rifle, and thumbed the hammer back.

Laughton glanced at her. He saw her ghastly face, saw both the terror and the determination in her eyes. His reaction was as automatic as that of a man ducking a blow. His hand went to the gun at his side.

He yanked it out and raised it, thumbing the hammer back.

Prudence fired, her reaction in doing so as automatic as Laughton's had been. He stopped, as if frozen into immobility, and a look of startled surprise came over his face. The revolver slipped from his hand and thudded to the ground, discharging from the impact.

Smoke curled from the muzzle of Prudence's gun. Slowly, deliberately, Laughton folded forward. His knees buckled before he hit the ground, and he collapsed in a heap, not a foot from the unconscious body of his wife. But before he fell, Prudence saw the bright red stain spreading on the front of his shirt.

Laughton's horse trotted nervously away, reins dragging on the ground. The buggy horse tried once more to bolt. He got no more than a dozen yards before Prudence hauled him to a stop.

For several moments she sat there numbly, unable to move, unable even to think. All of it had happened so very fast. She had not meant to shoot Laughton. She had raised the gun to threaten him, to make him let his wife alone. He, in turn, had reacted instinctively, and now he was dead and Prudence was a murderer.

She started violently when Mrs. Laughton appeared at the side of the buggy. The ranch woman's face was white with shock. Her dress was torn, the upper half of it scarcely covering her. Prudence whispered. "Is he . . . ?" and stopped.

Mrs. Laughton said numbly, "He's dead. My God, he's dead!"

Prudence climbed out of the buggy. Dazedly she clipped the tether weight to the bridle of the buggy horse. With Mrs. Laughton, she walked back to where Laughton lay.

His revolver was beside him, a faint wisp of smoke still curling up from the muzzle. Prudence said, "He would have shot me. He would have shot me if I hadn't fired first."

Mrs. Laughton stared at her, a strange expression in her eyes. Prudence said hysterically, "He would! You know he would!"

Mrs. Laughton finally nodded, but reluctantly. "He might." She studied Prudence a moment more. "What happened after he hit me and knocked me down?"

"He stooped over you. I was afraid. . . ." Tears now welled up in her eyes. "I thought he might. . . ." Again she stopped. "He was wild," she cried defensively. "I thought he might hurt you more or even

79

kill you! I raised the gun and screamed at him to stop. I didn't mean to shoot him. He grabbed for his own gun and I fired before he could. Even so, he fired it. You can see that if you'll look at it. He fired it!"

Her hysteria had mounted. Suddenly Mrs. Laughton put out a hand. "It's all right," she said. "It's all right. I know you didn't mean to shoot him."

Prudence's eyes were swimming with tears. She nodded numbly. "What are we going to do?"

"Lift him into the buggy. Take him in to town."

Prudence nodded. Together, and with some difficulty, they lifted Laughton's body and placed it in the buggy. Mrs. Laughton said, "If you'd rather not drive, you can ride his horse."

Prudence watched her climb into the buggy. She unclipped the tether weight and put it on the buggy floor. She did not look at Laughton's body but she couldn't help looking at his boots. There was a spot of blood on the toe of one of them.

She went to the horse Laughton had ridden here. He rolled his eyes at her, but she calmed him by stroking his nose and talking to him. He looked back at her wildly as she mounted, and she wondered if he'd try to buck her off. Apparently he wasn't used to a woman's skirts. She kept the reins tight so that he couldn't get his head down.

The buggy moved away and she fell in behind. And now, for the first time, she realized that she had eliminated another of the men she had sworn to kill.

The realization came to her as something of a shock and it gave her an eerie feeling that Laughton's death, and that of Gibbs, had happened much too easily. Was she getting help from some supernatural source?

She immediately put that disquieting thought out of her head. There was no supernatural source but the Almighty, and she wasn't willing to believe that He would condone or abet the taking of human life. No. It was just chance that she had been able to cause the deaths of both Gibbs and Laughton so easily and in so short a time.

Mrs. Laughton held the buggy horse to a steady trot all the way to town. The horse Prudence was riding seemed content to carry her after that first wild-eyed glance as she mounted him. They came into town in mid-afternoon and Mrs. Laughton drove straight to the sheriff's office. Prudence dismounted beside the buggy and tied the horse to the hitch rail in front of the jail.

Tate came to the door. He looked at Laughton's slumped body in the buggy and his glance went immediately to Prudence. He didn't speak to Mrs. Laughton but directed his question at Prudence. "What happened this time, Mrs. Dunson?"

Mrs. Laughton spoke before Prudence could answer him. "Can't we go inside? Can't you get someone to take him over to Eberly's?"

"Yes ma'am." The sheriff stepped away from the door. "Go on inside, ladies. I'll be in as soon as I can."

Prudence and Mrs. Laughton went into the sheriff's office. The sheriff closed the door. He climbed to the buggy seat and drove away in the buggy. He was gone about ten minutes, during which time both women sat silently, avoiding each other's eyes. Prudence wondered what Mrs. Laughton would say when the sheriff questioned her.

Tate returned. Face grave, he came in and closed the door. He looked at Prudence. "He had a bullet wound in the chest. Did you shoot him?"

Prudence nodded.

"Why?"

Prudence looked at Mrs. Laughton beseechingly. Mrs. Laughton said, "Mrs. Dunson came out to our place this morning and told me what had happened to her husband and to her. She told me James was one of the men responsible."

"And you believed her?"

"Yes I did. I know him, sheriff, and I know some of the things he has done in the past. I told Mrs. Dunson I intended leaving him and asked if I could ride to town with her. I told Howie Beech I was going and asked him to tell Mr. Laughton I would not be back. We weren't much more than half way to town when he caught up with us."

"And what happened then?"

"He ordered me to go back with him." Her tone was even, her calm enforced. "I refused. He yanked me out of the buggy and hit me with his fist. He would have done more but Mrs. Dunson ordered him to stop. She raised her gun to threaten him and I suppose he thought she was going to shoot. He pulled his gun but Mrs. Dunson fired first."

Tate glanced skeptically at Prudence. "Is that right?"

Prudence nodded.

"Exactly the way she's telling it?"

"Yes."

Tate got up and paced back and forth, a scowl on his face. He said, "Seems to me pretty damn strange the way these men you claim attacked your ranch are dying off."

"Are you going to arrest me?"

His scowl didn't fade. "I don't see how I can. But tell me this, Mrs. Dunson. How do you feel about killing James Laughton, even assuming you didn't kill Henry Gibbs? Seems to me a nice woman like you would feel kind of bad about taking human life."

Prudence stared at him as blankly as she could. She answered with a question of her own. "If the law had found him guilty of hanging Sam, what would have happened to him?"

"He'd probably have been hanged."

"Then he would have been dead. As punishment for his crime?"

"Yes."

"Would that have been so very much different from this?"

"You're damned right it would! It would all have been done legally!"

"Then why wasn't it done legally?"

Tate's face flushed. "I keep telling you," he said angrily, "that nobody's got the right to take the law into their own hands!"

"Not even if the law doesn't work? Not even if it lets killers get away?"

"Not even then! Maybe the law ain't perfect, but it's the only thing we got! If everybody breaks it whenever they feel disgusted with it, then we ain't got nothing at all!" He stopped, looked from one woman to the other, and then said disgustedly, "Oh hell, what's the use? You ladies can go. I'll let you know if there's anything else I need."

Prudence was glad to escape. Her conscience was troubling her. Fiercely she told herself that she was not going to give up. She was only doing what the law rightfully should have done.

Chapter 8

Howie Beech followed Laughton from the ranch purely out of curiosity; he wanted to see the confrontation between Laughton and his wife. Howie had worked as Laughton's chore man for nearly seven years and during that time he had taken considerable abuse. He figured Laughton's wife was the only person in the world who could give back to Laughton, in full measure, all the abuse he tried to heap on others. Howie wanted to be around to see it happen.

He stayed well behind Laughton and to one side, keeping himself at least partially concealed behind the low hills lying on the left side of the road.

He needn't have bothered. Not once did Laughton look around. He spurred his horse so savagely that Howie had trouble keeping up. He was still half a mile back when Laughton finally overtook the buggy and forced it to a halt.

Howie kept his horse at a run, wanting to get close. He wouldn't be able to hear anything that was said but he hoped to be able to see what Laughton did.

From slightly less than half a mile, he saw Laughton yank his wife from the buggy and dump her onto the ground. Laughton stooped to raise her up, but changed his mind, straightened, and went for his gun. Howie saw a puff of smoke and saw Laughton fall. But it was several seconds before the two reports reached his ears, the first unmistakably that of a rifle, the second, close on its heels, as unmistakably that of a revolver. Howie thought, "Lordy, the old son-of-a-bitch has been shot!"

Another woman climbed out of the buggy and helped Mrs. Laughton to her feet. The two stood there doing nothing for several minutes, apparently talking. Then they stooped and dragged Laughton's body to the buggy. Together, and with some difficulty, they lifted him in. The woman who had shot Laughton caught his horse and mounted him. Mrs. Laughton got into the buggy and drove toward town.

Beech sat his horse, staring after them, uncertain about what, if anything, he ought to do. Laughton was probably dead.

The fact that Mrs. Laughton was keeping the buggy horse at a trot was indication that there was no great hurry about getting him to town. Therefore, he must be dead.

That other woman in the buggy must have been Prudence Dunson, Howie thought. She had killed Henry Gibbs and gotten away with it, and now she had killed Laughton too. Howie supposed he ought to ride out to Shawcroft's ranch and tell him what had happened. Shawcroft would know what to do.

He turned his lathered, overheated horse, and angled toward the road. He walked and trotted the animal alternately, letting him cool gradually. When he finally reached Shawcroft's gate he opened it, rode through, then closed it behind. He headed down the lane toward the huge white house.

One of Shawcroft's hands hailed him as he rode into the yard. "Hello, Howie. What brings you 'way out here?"

"I got to see Mr. Shawcroft. It's important."

"He's in the barn."

Howie rode to the barn, dismounted, and went inside. Shawcroft was unsaddling a horse. He glanced at Howie inquiringly.

Howie said, "That Dunson woman's shot Mr. Laughton, Mr. Shawcroft."

"Shot him? When?"

"A little while ago. I seen it. She came out from town in a buggy an' talked to Mrs. Laughton an' pretty soon Mrs. Laughton told me to tell Mr. Laughton she was leavin' an' not comin' back. She got in the buggy an' the two of them drove away an' I went after Mr. Laughton. He ran 'em down an' got shot."

"Do you know how bad he's hurt?"

"I think he's dead. Them two women put him in the buggy an' headed off for town but they wasn't hurryin' like they would if he was only hurt."

Shawcroft was scowling. He said shortly, "All right, Howie. You did right. You go on back home now and do your chores."

"Yes sir." Howie lingered a moment, wanting something more but not really knowing what. Finally he turned and reluctantly returned to his horse. He mounted and rode toward home.

Shawcroft, scowling worriedly, watched him go. He yelled at the man who had first hailed Howie when he rode into the yard. "Get saddled and go over to Hardesty's. Tell him Laughton's been shot and to bring McAndrews and come over here."

89

The man hurried away toward the corral. Shawcroft called after him, "Do you know where Montoya is today?"

"Fixin' the windmill at Kiowa Springs."

"Go by there on your way to Hardesty's. Tell him I want him here."

"Yes sir." The man got a horse out of the corral, saddled, and rode away, kicking the horse into a lope.

Shawcroft watched him go. First Gibbs, he thought, and now Laughton. That damned woman wasn't as helpless as she looked. At least, in this case, there were witnesses. Howie Beech had seen her shoot Laughton and so had Laughton's wife. Maybe this time Tate would put the damn woman in jail and keep her there.

If the sheriff didn't . . . well, they'd take care of it themselves. He'd been thinking about doing something about all the settlers camped at the edge of town. Maybe it would work out so that he could get rid of them and the Dunson woman at the same time.

He turned his tired horse into the corral and caught himself another one. He saddled and then waited impatiently for Hardesty, McAndrews, and Montoya to arrive. But it was nearly four o'clock when he finally saw them coming.

Hardesty was wearing that ridiculous Confederate cavalry officer's hat, he noticed, the one that he was so damned fond of. Shawcroft wondered why the hell he didn't just forget the war the way everybody else had. The difference was, he supposed, that Hardesty had fought on the losing side. It was easier for the winners to forget the conflict than for those who have been licked. Besides that, Hardesty seemed to want people to know that he'd been a colonel. Brevet colonel, Shawcroft thought disparagingly. In peacetime brevet colonels were lucky if they were wearing second lieutenant's bars.

Hardesty, Montoya, and McAndrews galloped their horses into the yard. Hardesty asked, as if he was talking to a subordinate, "What's all this about Laughton being shot?"

"That's what Howie Beech said. Claims the Dunson woman shot him. I think it's time we did something about her."

"What do you suggest?"

"That we go to town and see Tate. If he's going to put her in jail maybe we won't have to do anything. But if he's going to let her off the hook, then we'd better figure something out. Maybe we can come up with a way to get rid of her and that

91

stinking bunch of settlers at the same time."

"All right. Let's go." Hardesty headed up the lane. Shawcroft mounted and followed him. McAndrews and Montoya lagged along worriedly, plainly concerned about getting in any deeper than they already were. Their stake in this was piddling compared to Shawcroft's and Hardesty's.

It was suppertime when they drew their horses to a halt in front of the jail. There was a smell of woodsmoke and of frying meat in the evening air. Shawcroft and Hardesty dismounted and went striding in. McAndrews and Montoya remained outside.

Tate was getting ready to go to supper, just putting on his hat. Hardesty asked in his best cavalry officer's voice, "Have you got that Dunson woman in jail?"

Tate's mouth tightened at Hardesty's tone. He shook his head.

"Why not? She killed Laughton, didn't she?"

"Yes. But she fired in self-defense. Mrs. Laughton was there and she confirms it. There will be a coroner's inquest tomorrow, and if Rufus says she ought to go to trial, then she'll go to trial."

"But there ain't much chance, right? Not

with Mrs. Laughton saying it was self-defense."

Tate nodded. "That's about it."

Shawcroft said furiously, "And it's open season on everybody that runs cattle around here. Is that what you're trying to say?"

"Not everybody that runs cattle," Tate said. "Looks like it's only open season on the ones that hanged Sam Dunson and burned out his place."

"Maybe it's time we did something about that damned woman ourselves."

Tate's voice had steel in it. "And maybe you've already done too much."

Hardesty uttered a single obscenity. He and Shawcroft turned and stamped out of the office, slamming the door thunderously.

Tate settled his hat on his head and followed them. Hardesty and Shawcroft mounted and thundered up the street to the saloon.

A couple of townsmen had to jump to get out of their way. From the safety of the walk they glared angrily at the backs of the two cowmen. Muttering, they turned away.

Tate watched all this uneasily. The mood of the town was changing, he thought. There was growing anger over the cowmen's arrogance, growing sympathy for the settlers who had been frightened off their land. If the town's resentment continued to intensify, there was trouble coming, because the cowmen were used to having things their way no matter what they had to do to make sure they did.

Hardesty and Shawcroft dismounted in front of the Drovers' Saloon and went in. Montoya and McAndrews, who had followed more slowly, stayed outside, hunkering down on their heels against the wall and rolling cigarettes.

Tate headed for the hotel. He didn't know whether to believe Prudence Dunson's story about Laughton's death or not. There was something funny about it. He sensed that in his bones. Mrs. Laughton hadn't been able to look him squarely in the eye as she told her version of it. She acted as if her story was rehearsed.

And Prudence Dunson. . . . She had been deathly pale when the two arrived in town and had trembled violently all the time he talked with her.

He cursed irritably beneath his breath. He wished she'd give up her stubborn quest for vengeance. She had killed two men and there was no way her conscience could cope successfully with that. She was too fine a woman to be able to kill and feel nothing afterward. Besides, if she kept on, she was either going to make a mistake and spend the next twenty years in prison, or get killed herself, or end up so bitter that the rest of her life would be completely spoiled.

But Tate could see no way of stopping her, unless, by some unlikely happenstance he was able to get one of the three hired hands who had participated in the hanging of her husband to talk.

Sourly, he went into the hotel, and sourly he found a chair. He didn't like his feeling of helplessness, but at the moment he couldn't think of anything he could do.

Shawcroft and Hardesty sat at a table in the Drovers' Saloon, a bottle between them. Both men were scowling, both trying to think of some way to get rid of Prudence Dunson and the settlers' camp at the edge of town.

Suddenly Shawcroft looked up. He glanced around to make sure nobody could overhear before he spoke guardedly. "I know what we can do."

"What?"

"Gather up a herd of Laughton's cattle. Hit that damn camp with 'em just at dawn.

There'll be so much dust and confusion nobody will be able to say who drove 'em there, and since they'll be Laughton's cattle, they won't be able to tie it in with us."

Hardesty brightened. "Good idea. But can we gather up a herd at night?"

"Sure we can. All we need is two or three hundred. You and me and Montoya and McAndrews and Finney will be all the help we need. Finney will know where the cattle are bedded down so we won't have to look all over hellangone for them."

"Let's get started then."

The two finished their drinks. Shawcroft left a dollar on the table. Outside, they untied and mounted and rode out of town. Montoya and McAndrews followed. Not until they had left the town behind did Shawcroft tell the pair about the plan.

Both Montoya and McAndrews looked uneasy, as if they would like to refuse. But they did not refuse. Both men liked their jobs, and in addition both knew they needed the protection of the two powerful cowmen if they wanted to avoid trouble over the Dunson attack.

The four rode steadily until they brought the Laughton place in sight. Three waited at the gate while McAndrews went in to find Finney. It was almost dark when he returned, with Finney riding a few paces behind.

Shawcroft outlined the plan swiftly. Then Finney led away, the other four following. It would take most of the night to gather up a herd and drive them to Broken Arrow so that they would be ready to run at dawn. If any of the five considered the possibility that women and children would be hurt or even killed, they gave no sign of it.

Chapter 9

Hector Hendricks got up while it was still dark. Stars winked in the early morning sky. He found a horse, saddled, mounted, and rode out of camp, leaving his parents and Mrs. Dunson, who had left the hotel and was staying at their camp again, asleep.

He had his father's rifle. He intended to try and kill an antelope and knew his best chance of getting one would be between dawn and the time the sun came up. There was a ridge about two miles from camp where, at dawn, there was usually a band of antelope. He planned to be there in place when it got light enough to shoot.

He reached the gully below the ridge while it still was dark. He dismounted and tied his horse to a clump of brush, then started up the side of the ridge afoot.

A strange low-pitched sound made him stop. Standing there motionless, he cocked his head, listening. The sound seemed to be both in the air and in the ground. He put his rifle butt on the ground, put the muzzle of the unloaded rifle in his ear. Listening this way he was able to pick up the rumble of approaching hoofs.

It puzzled him but it also irritated him. Someone had spoiled his morning's hunt. There was no longer any use creeping up the side of the ridge because the antelope would have been frightened away long before it was light enough to shoot.

He untied his horse. He never used cuss words in front of his folks, but he was using cuss words now. Some damn fool driving a large herd through the darkness toward him. He couldn't tell whether it consisted of horses or cattle, but no matter what the beasts were, it was puzzling. Why were they being driven at night? Why, unless someone was stealing them?

The thought of being discovered by rustlers frightened him. But curiosity temporarily got the better of his fright. He wanted to see the herd, wanted to see who was driving them and where they were headed.

The sound was plainer now, and suddenly he heard the low, distant bawling of a cow. Cattle, then, he thought. That made it almost certain that someone was stealing them.

Good sense got the best of curiosity. It was foolish to remain here in the path of the moving herd. He started back toward camp.

The sound diminished only slightly as he rode. He drew his horse to a walk and rode that way for a while. The sounds of the cattle neither faded nor grew louder.

Hector was really puzzled now because he realized that the herd was being driven straight toward them. That effectively ruled out the possibility that it was a stolen herd. But why was it being driven at night?

He kicked his horse into a trot and then a lope. The sound of the bawling herd diminished and finally faded altogether from his ears.

He rode into camp at a lope as the eastern horizon began to show a faint line of gray. His father was already up, as were many of the other settlers. Hector's father asked, "Get anything?"

"I didn't try. Somebody out there's driving a herd of cattle. I figured they'd have scared all the antelope away."

"Cattle? At night? Somebody must be rustling."

Hector shook his head. "I don't think so. They're heading straight toward town."

His father shrugged. "I guess it's no business of ours."

Hector got himself a cup of coffee. His father was right. Except for the fact that the drovers had done him out of his morning's hunt, it was no business of theirs.

Prudence Dunson overheard the conversation between Hector and his father. She was as puzzled as Hendricks over the herd being moved at night. But unlike Hendricks, she did not dismiss it from her mind. Cattle meant cattlemen. Cattlemen meant Shawcroft, Hardesty, and their hired hands. Shawcroft and Hardesty meant trouble for settlers. What better way, she thought, for them to get rid of both her and the settlers than to stampede a herd of cattle through their camp? Who could later tie them in with it?

She opened her mouth to tell Hendricks what she suspected, then closed it abruptly without saying anything. Men, even men with guns, would be helpless to turn a stampeding cattle herd.

A woman wouldn't, though. Not if she reached the herd before they actually began to run. Prudence had often chased cattle away from their plowed land and crops by simply screaming and flapping her apron or her skirts. She knew how terrified the half-wild beasts were of such unfamiliar things. And if she was wrong, if the herd was not headed for their camp, she would not have frightened the settlers unnecessarily.

She left quickly, heading away from camp in the direction from which Hector had entered it. She ran as swiftly as she could until she was out of breath.

She stopped and listened, and heard a low rumble that might have been either in the air, or in the ground, or both. They were coming then and she had probably been right. What she had to do now was reach them before their drovers made them stampede.

She ran again, directly toward the sound. Several times she tripped and fell, but each time she got up and hurried on. She wished now that she had warned those back in camp. She wished she had brought others to help her turn the cattle back. What if she wasn't successful in stampeding the cattle back in the direction from which they had come?

Too late for worrying, she thought. The sky was lighter now, and she could clearly see objects a hundred feet away.

Suddenly ahead, she saw a long, dark line of slowly moving cattle. They appeared to be a couple of hundred yards away, and she was almost squarely in their path.

She knelt, concealing herself behind a clump of brush as best she could. Her best chance of frightening them would be, she knew, by appearing suddenly. If they were sufficiently startled, and if she screeched and flapped her skirts enough, perhaps they'd turn back, or at least turn aside.

The cold-bloodedness of the cattlemen's action appalled her. And yet why should she be appalled? Hadn't they hanged Sam, knowing him to be innocent?

Closer and closer the cattle came. A huge dust cloud rose behind them, almost concealing their drovers, who looked, in the boiling dust, like wraiths.

It was time. The cattle were less than a hundred feet away. If she waited any longer she'd only spook those in the center of the line. The others wouldn't see her at all.

She jumped to her feet, let out the best scream she could, and it was a good one. It stopped the line of cattle as if they had run into some kind of invisible wall.

Prudence screamed again. As she did,

she stooped and seized her skirt about halfway to the hem. She began to flap it violently with her hands, screeching and running forward as she did.

She could see the cattle's eyes — open wide, whites showing — and she could see their flaring nostrils and their sharp-pointed horns. For one terrible instant she thought that, instead of turning and running away from her, they were going to charge.

Behind them, pistol shots barked as the drovers attempted to force them to stampede over her. Prudence let out a shriek even better than the first had been. Tearing off her apron, she raised it over her head, flapping it wildly as she did.

One big steer in front snorted and pawed the ground. Then, so suddenly that it startled her, he turned tail and rammed his head and horns into the packed mass in back of him.

His sudden action was all it took. Almost like one animal, the first eight or ten rows turned tail. Those in the back were slower turning, but they couldn't stand against the awful force of the terrified beasts in front.

In less than a minute it was all over. The herd was in full thundering flight, now away from Prudence, who stood looking small and helpless in the blinding cloud of dust.

Pistol shots were insignificant popping sounds. The yells of the drovers were lost in the crescendo of noise. The ground shook beneath the pounding hoofs. The air trembled with the bawling of five hundred terrified half-wild animals. Horns struck horns as each beast fought to get ahead of the one in front of him.

Appalled, Prudence stared after the retreating herd. The drovers, who had long since stopped trying to turn the cattle back, now rode in the midst of them, attempting to work their way to the edge of the herd, from where they might have a chance of overtaking the leaders and turning them aside. The whole boiling mass quickly disappeared from Prudence's sight and only the towering, choking, blinding cloud of dust remained.

The rumble of hoofs and the bawling diminished and faded, even as the dust cloud dispersed on the early morning breeze. Then Prudence was alone, in almost complete silence.

She turned and plodded back toward camp.

Sheriff Jason Tate heard the distant

pistol shots. He heard the bawling of five hundred cattle and he heard the rumble in the ground as they began to run.

Without even taking time to close the office door, he sprinted for the livery stable. He bridled the first horse he found and leaped to the animal's back without bothering to saddle him. He knew what the shots and bawling were about, or thought he did. The cattlemen had picked this way of getting rid of Prudence Dunson and the settlers camped out at the edge of town.

But the camp, when he reached it, was intact. The settlers, instead of fleeing, were walking out across the prairie toward a brown dust cloud about half a mile away.

Tate turned his horse and rode after them, kicking the animal into a lope. He overtook the settlers and passed them, and shortly afterward he encountered Prudence Dunson, covered with dust but unhurt, walking slowly toward town.

He hauled his horse to a plunging halt. "I might have known it would be you," he said accusingly.

Her eyes snapped as she looked up at him. "What do you mean, you might have known it would be me? I didn't raise all that dust. I didn't make all that noise. They meant to kill us all! They were going to stampede that herd right through our camp!"

"But you ran out here and stopped them." Disbelief was thick in his voice.

"That's exactly what I did."

"How did you know they were here?"

"Hector. He went out to hunt antelope and heard them coming in the dark. He rode back to camp and told his father. I overheard and guessed what the herd was for. I was right, too. They were headed straight toward our camp."

Tate nodded. "All right, Mrs. Dunson. Go back to camp. I'll see if I can catch up with them and find out who they are."

She studied him spiritedly. "I'm glad to know the law is finally going to do something."

"Yes ma'am," he said dryly, and turned his horse away from her. He kicked the horse into a lope again, following the trail left by the stampeding herd.

The dust cloud seemed to move ahead of him. He rode for three miles before he saw a riderless horse well to his left. The horse's reins were dragging on the ground, and the animal was unconcernedly cropping grass.

Tate rode to the horse and looked at it. The animal wore Laughton's brand on his hip. He was dripping with sweat, his neck lathered. Though he was calm now, his legs were still trembling.

Tate stared back along the pounded trail left by the stampeding cattle. Whoever had ridden that horse was down. Tate thought he knew what he was going to find. This horse's rider had fallen off, probably in the middle of the stampede. It was extremely doubtful if he had survived.

Slower now, leading the riderless horse, Tate returned to the beaten trail. He followed it back toward town for a mile before he saw the lumped shape on the ground ahead of him.

The horse pulled back, rolled his eyes, and laid back his ears as Tate drew near. He circled, to come up on the dead man from upwind. When he was a dozen yards away, he dismounted. He dropped both horses' reins upon the ground.

The body was that of Luke Finney, who had been Laughton's foreman when Laughton was alive. He was almost unrecognizable from being pounded by the cattle's hoofs.

Without touching the body, Tate mounted and rode back toward town, still leading Finney's horse. There was a growing, uneasy chill in his spine.

Prudence Dunson had sworn to kill the seven men who had hanged her husband, burned her house, and caused her to lose her child. Only five days had passed and three were already dead. In each case, Prudence Dunson had been directly responsible.

It was eerie and it was frightening. It made Sheriff Tate wish he was anywhere but here.

Chapter 10

When Tate got back to town, he sent Rufus
Gant out to pick up Finney's body. He told
Rufus he'd just as well combine the inquests
into the deaths of Laughton and Finney.
Laughton's inquest had been set for eleven
o'clock and there was no reason Gant
couldn't be back before that time.

Gant arrived with Finney's body, wrapped
in canvas, about ten o'clock. Shortly afterward Shawcroft and Hardesty rode angrily
into town. They hauled their lathered
horses to a halt, stepped down, and
stormed into the sheriff's office. Hardesty
was wearing his Confederate officer's hat.
It was covered with dust, as was the rest of
him. He stopped just inside the door,
ramrod straight, as befitted a Confederate
colonel, and barked, "Sheriff Tate! By
God, sir, what are you going to do about
that confounded woman? She is directly
responsible for Finney's death and this

time there is no chance you can explain her actions away."

Tate didn't get up out of his chair. "Didn't plan to try," he said. "She admits she stampeded them cattle."

"Then arrest her! She has some kind of ridiculous idea that we killed her husband, but it simply isn't true. I for one want her in jail before she succeeds in killing any more of us!"

"She says those cattle were headed straight for the settlers' camp. Were they?"

"No sir! They were not! They were headed toward town."

"Why? People don't generally ship cattle in the spring."

For an instant, Hardesty seemed at a loss for words. He swallowed and glanced at Shawcroft. Shawcroft said, "We were just helping Mrs. Laughton out. We knew she wasn't going to be able to run that ranch all by herself. We figured she'd want to sell off some of her stock." It was a ridiculously unlikely story, told lamely, and Tate said, "You're both liars. You were doing exactly what Mrs. Dunson says you were. Now get out of here. If you want to attend the inquest, you're free to do so. Tell Rufus that ridiculous story and see if he believes it any more than I do."

Hardesty blustered, "You'll be sorry for this, sir!"

"Maybe. See you at the inquest." He watched them mount their horses and ride away. He went out, untied his own horse, and rode straight to the settlers' camp.

Prudence Dunson glanced up as he approached. He asked bluntly, "Did you know that a man was killed in that cattle stampede?"

He thought her face lost color. Then her color returned and her eyes took on a defiant look. "That is too bad, sheriff. Who was the man?"

"Finney. Laughton's foreman."

"He was one of those who helped hang Sam."

Tate said brutally, "He makes three. Now you have only four to go."

She didn't answer that. He said, "The inquests for both Laughton and Finney will be held in half an hour, in case you want to attend."

"Why should I attend?"

"You killed them. I thought maybe you'd be interested."

"You mean you thought I might want to gloat?"

He could see that he had hurt her and he supposed he had wanted to. Some way he had to talk her out of going on. She was building up enough guilt to ruin her entire life. Maybe it already was too late. He said, "Mrs. Dunson, don't go on with this."

"I'm afraid I don't know what you mean."

Tate shrugged. "Have it your way." He turned his horse and rode back toward town.

Prudence Dunson watched him. She felt no elation over Finney's death. He had helped kill Sam and she had sworn vengeance against all those who had, but for some reason she felt no triumph at having caused Finney's death.

Like Tate, she was beginning to feel an overwhelming awe at the way things were happening. Three of the men she had sworn to kill were dead, and in one way she was directly responsible for their deaths. Yet their deaths had really been caused by their own actions. Gibbs had panicked because of his guilt. Laughton's own violence had caused his death. Finney was dead because he had joined the others in trying to wipe out the settlers' camp. Neither Finney nor the others had cared how many innocent lives would have been lost had they been successful in stampeding their five hundred cattle through the camp.

Maybe, though, Sheriff Tate was right. Maybe she shouldn't go on with it. Maybe Sam wouldn't have wanted her to go on with it.

On impulse, she got a bridle from Hendricks' wagon and carried it to the grove of trees where the horses were. She caught one of Olaf Hendricks' wagon horses and put the bridle on. She led him to a bank where she could mount, and got on bareback. With her skirts pulled up, she rode astride and headed toward the homestead where she and Sam had lived. Maybe, she thought, if she went out there she would know what she should do. Maybe if she could look at the place where it had happened something would tell her whether she should stop or go on.

Physically, she felt better than she had since that terrible night. She was young and strong and had recovered quickly from the aftereffects of her miscarriage. But her state of mind had not improved. She was as depressed and unhappy as she had been immediately afterward. Her life stretched away before her, gray and bleak and without hope. She didn't care about the land she and Sam had worked so hard to earn. She cared nothing for the livestock they had acquired at such great sacrifice.

Her vengeance was all she had. Without it she might as well be dead.

She reached the place in early afternoon. She rode first to the blackened rubble of the house, and almost reluctantly slid off the horse.

She discovered that she couldn't even visualize the house the way it once had been. She walked to the shovel Olaf Hendricks had stuck into the ground to mark Sam's grave. She knelt. She let the silence of the prairie wash over her. She closed her eyes. She wanted to pray but she had the feeling it would be a blasphemy to bring God into what she was doing. The commandments were clear enough and she was deliberately breaking them. At least she was breaking one.

When her voice came, it was a cry of agony. "Sam! Tell me what to do!"

Only the vast silence of the prairie answered her.

She remained, kneeling, her eyes shut, for a long time. Slowly a kind of calm came over her. It was as if Sam had reassured her from the grave. Finally she got up. She walked to the place where she had buried what would eventually have been their child.

She stood over it, looking down, bitterness now coming back to her. Would the child have been a boy or girl? And if a boy, would he have been like Sam? Her face twisted with anguish. Why couldn't they have left her the child at least? Why?

She was finished here. She walked back to the horse. She led it down to the gully where a small stream of water ran, and mounted from a bank. Without a backward glance, she rode back toward town. She didn't know how the answers she had sought had come to her. She only knew they had. She would go on, if not in the name of vengeance, then to assure that the same kind of thing wouldn't happen to any other settlers. With Shawcroft and Hardesty gone, the settlers now camped at the edge of town could move back out onto their claims.

The coroner's inquest went much as Sheriff Tate had expected that it would. Rufus Gant took up the matter of Laughton's death first. He called Mrs. Laughton to give testimony, and in response to his questions she told her story, about how she had decided to leave her husband when Prudence Dunson told her what he had done.

Gant asked, "How was it that you were so willing to believe the word of a total stranger? Didn't it occur to you that she might not be telling the truth?"

"No sir. It didn't."

"Why not?"

"Because this was not the first time he had taken the law into his own hands."

"When were the other times?"

"Back about ten years ago he caught three men rustling cattle from him. One wasn't any more than twelve or thirteen years old. But he hanged them all, the boy included."

"Why didn't you leave him then?"

"We had been losing a lot of cattle. He had asked the law for help but the sheriff — not Mr. Tate — told him he'd have to take care of it himself. He did."

"And there were other times?"

"Yes. He and his crew attacked a small Indian camp not much more than a year afterward. I don't know how many they killed, because he would never tell, but it must have been quite a lot because he kept guards around the house at night for a year afterward."

"Then what Mrs. Dunson told you was just the last straw?"

"Yes sir. I told him a couple of years ago when he and Mr. Shawcroft hanged a horse thief that I wasn't going to stand for any more. I told him we had law here now and that when something happened he was to take it to the law."

"So you sent Howie Beech to tell him you had gone?"

"Yes sir. And that I was not coming back."

"Go on please, Mrs. Laughton. Tell it in your own words."

"He overtook us. He stopped beside the buggy and began to yell at me. He demanded that I return home with him at once. I refused and he yanked me from the buggy. When I tried to get up, he hit me with his fist."

"Did the blow knock you out?"

"It stunned me." For the first time, Mrs. Laughton was hesitant.

"Did it knock you out? By that I mean did you lose consciousness?"

It was several moments before Mrs. Laughton replied. When she did, she raised her head defiantly. Looking squarely at Gant she said clearly, "No, I did not."

Sheriff Tate knew she was lying. He also knew he'd never make her admit it, and he wasn't sure he wanted to.

Gant asked, "And then what happened?"

"He stooped to grab me again. Mrs. Dunson screamed at him to stop. He looked at her and saw that she had a rifle in her hands, and I suppose he thought she meant to shoot. He grabbed for his own gun."

"And Mrs. Dunson fired?"

"Yes sir." Mrs. Laughton's voice, now, was almost inaudible.

Gant said, "All right, Mrs. Laughton. Thank you."

The inquest into the death of Finney went more slowly. Gant questioned Mc-Andrews, Montoya, Shawcroft, and Hardesty. Each told substantially the same story, that they had been driving a herd of Laughton cattle to town to sell. When asked who the prospective buyer was, none of the four could give an answer. When asked why they were driving the herd at night, all said lamely that since it was cooler the cattle would lose less weight. Their performance was such that every person in the hotel lobby, which was serving as a courtroom, knew they were lying. Gant called Mrs. Laughton to the stand.

"Did you know these men were moving your cattle into town to be sold?"

"No sir, I did not. They had no authorization from me."

"What about Mr. Finney? Did he have

the authority to sell cattle for you?"

"No sir. He did not."

"Thank you, Mrs. Laughton."

Mrs. Laughton left the stand. Rufus Gant said, "I find the death of Mr. Finney to be accidental. I find that Mr. Laughton died at the hands of Prudence Dunson and that Prudence Dunson was acting in self-defense."

Shawcroft, Hardesty, McAndrews, and Montoya grumbled at the decision, but the townspeople and settlers approved it excitedly and noisily. Tate sat still until everyone had left.

Then he walked to Rufus Gant. Gant asked, "Verdict suit you?"

Tate nodded. Gant asked, "Who do you reckon will be next?"

"I don't think anyone will be. I think she's going to quit."

"Maybe she won't have no choice. She didn't have much choice when they headed that bunch of cattle toward the settlers' camp."

Tate shrugged. Gant said, "The settlers are talking about moving back out onto their land. You know what will happen if they do."

Tate knew. He said, "I'll try to keep an eye on them."

But he knew there wasn't much that he could do. There were six or eight settler families in the camp at the edge of town. If they all moved back out onto their claims . . . well, he couldn't watch them all.

And Shawcroft and Hardesty, threatened and with their backs to the wall, weren't going to consider letting them alone.

Tate wished he had a dozen deputies. But he only had himself.

Chapter 11

Tate was right about the settlers moving back onto their land as a result of the coroner's verdict. They began packing up as soon as they got back to camp, and by the time darkness fell, most of them were ready to go, waiting only for daylight tomorrow.

Olaf Hendricks, his wife, and his son Hector were among those ready to go at dawn. Prudence Dunson had helped them all the previous afternoon, but when Hendricks extended an invitation to her to come and stay with them, she refused. She didn't want to be responsible for anything that happened, and she felt that her presence at the Hendricks place would only insure they would be the first family attacked.

In the first early light, she watched the exodus. Within an hour, the settlers' camp at the edge of town was vacant, littered with the refuse of their presence, with the blackened remains of their campfires, the discarded toys of their children, the manure of their animals.

Slowly, Prudence walked back into town, carrying her belongings in an old carpetbag Mrs. Hendricks had given her. She had the uneasy feeling that if anything happened to any of the settlers, she would feel responsible, since her actions had given them the courage to return.

Tate saw her walking up Shoshoni Street and came out of the sheriff's office to stand in the morning sun squinting at her. He nodded. "Morning, Mrs. Dunson."

"Good morning, sheriff."

He asked, "Where are you going to stay?"

"The hotel, I suppose."

"What about your feud with the cattlemen?"

"What feud, sheriff?"

He shrugged. "All right." He studied her closely as he said, "Think about it, Mrs. Dunson. Think what Sam would have wanted you to do. He wouldn't have insisted on the kind of vengeance you're trying for. You're going to end up hurting yourself."

She smiled faintly. "Thank you, sheriff."

"For what?"

"For caring what happens to me. I'll think about what you've said." She went on up the street toward the hotel and he watched her until she disappeared inside. Maybe she really would quit, he thought, and go away. Strangely, that prospect made him no happier than having her stay and continue her feud with the cattlemen.

McAndrews rode into the Hardesty home place in mid-afternoon. Hardesty was in the big corral, schooling a thoroughbred. He was wearing his Confederate officer's hat, and in his hand he had a riding crop. He looked at McAndrews questioningly.

McAndrews was a burly, red-haired man who looked as if he might have been Hardesty's sergeant in the war. He said, "The whole damn bunch is back. I checked every homestead on our range and some of those on Shawcroft's range."

Hardesty's eyes were cold, his mouth a thin, straight line. In his best military tone he snapped, "Ride over to Shawcroft's place. Tell him to meet me here right away. I guess it's time we taught those squatters a lesson they won't forget."

McAndrews looked at him doubtfully. Hardesty barked, "Don't sit there staring at me like an idiot! I've given you an order!"

McAndrews ducked his head. Grumbling something Hardesty couldn't hear, he wheeled his horse and rode away, back in the direction from which he had come. At the gate, he turned toward Shawcroft's ranch.

Hardesty sat staring after him, a fierce scowl on his face. He had the uneasy feeling that he was going to have trouble with McAndrews. Montoya might give them trouble too. Both were superstitious fools. They thought there was something supernatural in the three deaths Prudence Dunson had caused. They were wondering who of the four remaining would be next.

He tried going on with schooling the thoroughbred but he couldn't keep his mind on it so he finally dismounted, led the spirited animal into the barn, and took the saddle off. He rubbed the horse down and put him into a stall. He gave him a measure of oats.

After that, he paced nervously back and forth, occasionally striking his boot top with the riding crop. Time dragged, but at last he saw three riders coming down the lane. It was nearly sundown.

The three rode straight to the barn, dismounted, and came inside. Hardesty looked at Shawcroft's untidy white hair with faint disapproval. He asked, "Did McAndrews tell you?"

Shawcroft nodded.

Hardesty said, "We've got to do something. Tonight. If we let those stinking settlers stay one night out there it's going to be just that much harder getting them to leave."

Montoya wore an uneasy look. He asked, "What you plan, Mr. Hardesty?"

Hardesty glanced at him impatiently, his look saying it was unseemly for hired hands to question their employers about anything. The look softened quickly as he realized how much he and Shawcroft needed these two hired hands. He said grudgingly, "Hendricks is their backbone. If we hit his place, they'll all skeedaddle. Only this time they won't stay in town. They'll leave the country for good."

McAndrews asked suspiciously, "What do you mean, exactly, by 'hit the Hendricks place'?"

"What do you think, for Christ's sake? Wipe 'em out. Burn everything."

"You mean to kill the woman too?"

"Yes, by God. If we'd killed that damned Dunson woman when we hit her place we wouldn't have all this trouble now."

McAndrews glanced at Montoya, then back at Hardesty. He said firmly, "No sir. Not me. I ain't going to be part of killing no womenfolk."

Hardesty's face turned an angry red, his

126

mouth tightened. He said sharply, "You'll do what I tell you to!"

"No sir. Not this."

Hardesty swung the riding crop. It struck McAndrews in the mouth and blood ran from his lips and down his chin.

He lunged at Hardesty, his eyes like those of a charging bull. Hardesty cut him across the face a second time with the riding crop, stepping back afterward to avoid the nearly blind and thoroughly maddened man. McAndrews roared, "You blowed-up son-of-a-bitch!"

Hardesty, equally angry, barked back, "You insubordinate dog! I'll. . . ."

McAndrews, having rushed past Hardesty, now turned. Hardesty still held only the riding crop. McAndrews glanced to right and left for a weapon that would even things. A pitchfork was sticking in the dry manure that covered the floor. He seized it and raised it like a spear.

Shawcroft roared, "Mac! Put that damned thing down!"

McAndrews didn't seem to hear. He drew back the fork preparatory to hurling it.

Smoke billowed from the gun in Shawcroft's hand. The report was deafening in this enclosed space. Back in the stalls, horses snorted, reared, and tried to pull loose.

McAndrews switched his glance to Shaw-croft, surprise having replaced the fury on his face. The pitchfork still was poised. A red stain began to spread on the front of his shirt.

Shawcroft said, "Hardesty, if you'd forget just one damn time about the rank you held during the war! Now look what you've done!"

Hardesty turned his head. "What *I've* done? I didn't shoot him. You did."

McAndrews still had not fallen. He was obviously maintaining his upright position with difficulty. He suddenly dropped the pitchfork and swayed.

Montoya moved forward and propped him up. Outside the barn, up at the house, a woman's voice shrilled, "Don? Was that a shot?"

Hardesty pulled his fascinated glance from the front of McAndrews' shirt. He walked to the barn door with the jerky steps of a sleepwalker. He called, "Damn gun went off accidentally. No harm done."

He came walking back. Shawcroft stood on the other side of McAndrews, helping Montoya to keep him upright, but it was no use. McAndrews' legs buckled and he sagged. Shawcroft and Montoya eased him

128

down onto the floor.

Hardesty said, "He's dead."

Shawcroft knelt and put his ear against McAndrews' chest. He raised up and nodded numbly, "I did it to save your life. He'd have got you with that fork."

The sight of death was nothing new to Hardesty and it didn't move him except for the fact that McAndrews had worked for him a long, long time. He said, "It's done. Now what we got to figure is how to get out of it."

"We'll just tell Tate what happened."

"Don't be a damn fool. What will we tell him the argument was about?"

Shawcroft was silent. Montoya was looking from Hardesty to Shawcroft and back again. There was growing uneasiness in his eyes.

Hardesty said, "Montoya, go catch that buckskin team in the corral. Bring them in here and we'll harness them to the buckboard. When it gets dark, we'll take McAndrews into town. We'll take him upstairs and leave him in that Dunson woman's room. Then let's see her get out of that."

Montoya hurried away. Shawcroft's hands were shaking. He sat down on an overturned nail keg. After a while he glanced up. "Damn you, if you hadn't cut

129

him with that stinking fancy quirt."

"But I did. And you did. And there's nothing to be gained by putting blame."

"I guess not."

Montoya brought the team. The sun was down now, staining the clouds a brilliant orange. Hardesty said, "Harness is over there. Buckboard's in the back of the barn. I'm going up to the house and tell Martha I'm going into town."

He disappeared. Shawcroft helped Montoya harness the buckskin team. Montoya drove them to the rear of the barn and hitched them to a buckboard. He climbed to the seat and drove to where McAndrews lay. He got down. "Help me lift him in."

Shawcroft helped, not looking at McAndrews' face. When McAndrews' body was in the buckboard, Shawcroft looked at Montoya miserably. "I didn't want to shoot him. I liked the man. But he'd have drove that pitchfork through Hardesty if I hadn't."

"Yes sir." There was no conviction in Montoya's voice.

Hardesty returned, carrying a dark blanket. He spread it over the body in the back. Then he climbed to the seat. "Put your horses in the corral. Put Mac's horse in there too."

Shawcroft and Montoya led the three

horses away. They returned shortly, and silently climbed to the buckboard seat.

Hardesty drove out. His wife came to the kitchen door and watched him drive out of the yard. Shawcroft asked, "She suspect anything?"

"No. I told her I needed salt."

"Funny time to be going after it."

"I told her I was going to spend the night in town and bring it out in the morning."

After that, they drove in silence. The gray in the sky faded and became a velvet black. Stars winked out.

The town was quiet when they arrived. The supper hour was long since past, and it was still a little early for the saloons to be going good. Hardesty took the alley behind Shoshoni Street. When he reached the rear door of the hotel, he told Montoya, "Go around front and find out what room she's in. Come through to the back and unlock the door for us."

Montoya climbed down and disappeared. Hardesty said, "He's scared. Can you trust him?"

Shawcroft said, "He's worked for me fifteen years. If I can't trust him, I don't know who I can."

"McAndrews had worked for me a long time too. That didn't stop him from trying to kill me with a filthy fork."

Shawcroft said, "You push a man. It's a wonder one of your men didn't kill you during the war."

Surprisingly, that made Hardesty defensive. "I was a good officer."

"Sure. Sure you were. What battles were you in, anyway?"

There suddenly was a strange quality to Hardesty's voice. "Antietam. Bull Run, first and second. The Wilderness."

Shawcroft didn't reply. He didn't seem to be listening. To himself he muttered softly, "Christ, if I only hadn't had that gun."

The back door of the hotel opened and Montoya came out. Shawcroft and Montoya lifted McAndrews out, wrapped in the blanket. Hardesty went ahead, to hold the door for them.

They carried the body up the rear stairs and down the hall to Prudence Dunson's room. Montoya had the key and had ascertained that she was not inside the room. They left him lying face up, eyes open, in the middle of the floor. Hurrying back down the rear stairs and out the back door, they got up on the buckboard seat and drove away.

Hardesty took the buckboard to the livery stable. Then the three headed for the saloon.

Chapter 12

Prudence Dunson, having had supper in the hotel dining room, returned to her room no more than twenty minutes after Montoya, Shawcroft, and Hardesty had left. She inserted her key, surprised when the door opened without her having to turn the key. She hesitated a moment, scoffing at her own uneasiness, then pushed the door open.

There were lamps burning at intervals along the hall, secured by brackets to the wall. Although the light was dim, it was enough for her to see the body on the floor. She didn't scream, but the sound of her quickly indrawn breath would have been audible to anyone in the upstairs hall.

She closed the door and walked quietly to the stairs. She hurried down, across the lobby, and out into the night. Once in the street she ran, straight toward the sheriff's office.

She was out of breath when she burst inside. Tate glanced up from his desk, surprised. She said breathlessly, "Sheriff, there is a dead man in my room."

He opened his mouth to ask her if she was sure, closed it without saying anything. He got to his feet. "Let's go take a look."

Together they hurried along the street to the hotel. Tate led the way up the stairs. He opened Prudence's door, went in, and lighted the lamp. Prudence stayed outside until he said, "You can come in now, Mrs. Dunson."

She went in, to find that he had covered the body with a blanket from the bed. She stared in horror at the covered shape. "Who is it?"

"McAndrews." Tate was studying her suspiciously. "Are you sure you don't know anything about this?"

"Of course I don't. Do you think I would be foolish enough to kill someone in my room and then come running to you about it?"

Tate said sourly, "I don't honestly know what you'd do."

"Well, I didn't kill him. And if I didn't, then he must have been carried here. Aren't there ways of telling how long he has been dead?"

Tate nodded. He knelt beside the body

on the floor and drew the blanket back. He put his hand on McAndrews' neck and found it cold. McAndrews had to have been dead for a couple of hours. Something on the floor drew Tate's glance. He shoved the body slightly to one side so that he could examine it. It was a fine, dry powder that he recognized as manure. He rolled the body onto its side and discovered that the powdered manure was all over McAndrews' back. He covered the body again and got to his feet. "He's been dead for quite a while because he's cold. There's manure all over his back so he must have been killed either in a barn or a corral. I'd guess a barn."

"Then you're satisfied that I had nothing to do with his death?"

"I'm satisfied. I'm also satisfied that they'll go to considerable lengths to get rid of you. I wish you'd get out of town before something like this happens to you."

"I think it would be better if you worried about the settlers."

Tate stared patiently at her. "I am worried about them. But there's only one of me. I can't be every place at once."

They stared coldly at each other for a moment. Finally Tate said, "You can wait in the lobby. I'll get some men to remove this body and I'll ask Mrs. Jellico to have your room cleaned up."

"Thank you." She went out and Tate followed her. Going down the stairs, Prudence said, "I am not in any way responsible for that man's death." She was a little surprised to discover that she wanted Jason Tate to think well of her.

He growled, "Maybe you're not directly responsible but it's because of you he's dead."

Anger touched her. "How can you say a thing like that? It's because of their attack on our home that he is dead. I didn't start this, sheriff. Maybe you should remember that." She hadn't meant to sound quite so sharp but she was defiant enough not to care.

He did not reply. As he left her in the lobby he said, "I'll get this done as quickly as I can."

She halted him. "What are you going to do about the settlers? Nothing?"

Tate looked at her wearily. "Ma'am, there's nothing I *can* do. I got about all I can do watching you."

"I don't need to be watched."

"The hell you don't! You got that bunch scared, what's left of them. If you didn't, they wouldn't have bothered to dump a body in your room. Do you seriously think they won't try killing you if they think that's what it's going to take to save their own precious necks?"

Prudence said, "They will be more likely to attack the Hendricks place because of the Hendricks' friendship with me. You only need to watch the Hendricks family."

"No. Now, dammit, quit pesterin' me!"

"Very well, sheriff. I suppose I'll have to go to the Hendricks place myself."

"You stay away from there!"

"I will not! I intend going out there the first thing tomorrow."

He scowled angrily at her. Then he turned on his heel and stalked to the door.

Prudence sat down on one of the ancient, leather-covered sofas. Her threat had been a spur-of-the-moment thing, but now that she had made it she knew she would have to go through with it. Which might not be such a bad thing; if Jason Tate was as concerned about her safety as he claimed to be, he'd follow her and maybe he'd keep an eye on the Hendricks place. And by doing so maybe he'd catch the cattlemen when they tried to burn Hendricks out.

Tate returned with a stretcher and a couple of men. While they went upstairs for the body, Tate sought out Mrs. Jellico, who took a new blanket up along with a dustpan and broom with which to clean the floor. The men came down the stairs with McAndrews' body on the stretcher, still covered with the blanket from Prudence's bed.

Prudence headed up the stairs. Anne Jellico met her in the hall. "Don't you want another room?" she asked.

Prudence nodded. She'd have tried sleeping in her old room but she was relieved to find it would not be necessary. Besides, it might be just as well if the men who had put the body there didn't know where she was.

She got her bag and went into the room Mrs. Jellico assigned to her. She said good night and carefully locked the door. She got undressed and went to bed, but every time she closed her eyes she saw that awkwardly sprawled body lying on the floor of her room.

For the first time since the awful night when Sam was killed, she was scared. She felt cold with fear. Sheriff Tate was right; they *would* try to kill her. It was possible that they wanted her dead even more than they wanted to be rid of the settlers.

It was nearly midnight before she went

to sleep. Even then her sleep was tormented by uneasy dreams and frequent awakenings. She was glad to see the dawn.

She got up as soon as it was light enough to see. She dressed herself and packed everything in her bag in case she decided to stay at the Hendricks place that night. She went out and down the stairs.

It was too early for the hotel dining room, but she wasn't hungry anyway. She found a sleepy-eyed hostler at the livery stable and had him hitch a horse to a buggy for her. She drove out of the stable just as the rising sun began staining the high clouds in the east.

She was startled to find Sheriff Tate waiting in the street for her. She asked, "What are you doing out so early, sheriff?"

"Waiting for you. I'm going with you."

"That will not be necessary." She tried not to let her relief show.

"Maybe not, but I'm going anyway. Are you going to let me ride in the buggy or do I have to follow you?"

She gave him a faint smile. "I suppose you can ride with me if you want to."

He nodded. He dismounted and tied his horse behind her buggy. He climbed in and she handed him the reins. He slapped the horse's back with them and drove out of town, heading toward the Hendricks place.

Prudence felt ill at ease with Tate and wondered why. She glanced sideways at him, and suddenly his face, in profile, reminded her of Sam. It had the same strong lines, the same jutting jaw. She realized that she liked Jason Tate and that was why she had wanted him to think well of her.

She asked, "Do you have any ideas about why they killed Mr. McAndrews?"

The sheriff said, "They must've got to squabbling among themselves."

"Enough to start killing each other?"

"Maybe the killing wasn't intentional. Could've been a fight."

"A fight about what?"

"Probably what to do about you. Maybe what to do if the settlers moved back out onto the land."

"What do *you* think they'll do?"

"Likely they'll try scaring the settlers off again."

"And start with the Hendricks?"

Tate shook his head. "Too obvious. They'll figure I'm watching the Hendricks family. They'll also figure that some of the other settlers are staying with Hendricks just waiting for them to come. No. They'll hit someplace where nobody's expecting them."

"If you know that why aren't you doing something?"

Wearily Tate said, "Mrs. Dunson, I'd like nothing better. But I haven't even got a deputy. The county commissioners are too stingy to pay for one."

For the first time, Prudence considered the sheriff's side of this. She had been unfair to him. He wasn't on the side of the cattlemen. He wasn't even on the side of the settlers. He was just trying to enforce the laws and keep the peace. He'd have arrested the cowmen for killing Sam if it would have done any good. She said, "I'm sorry. I guess I haven't been very fair to you."

He shrugged. "That's understandable. This whole thing hasn't been easy for you. How long are you going to stay at the Hendricks place?"

She smiled ruefully. "I don't know. The only reason I came today was because I felt sure you would follow me. Now that you've convinced me the Hendricks family won't be hurt, I don't know what I'll do."

"If you want to leave the country, I'll see to it that your stock is gathered up and sold and I'll send the money on to you."

"Maybe that's what I'll do." But she didn't want to leave. She didn't know where she'd go if she did.

They brought the Hendricks homestead in sight a little after nine o'clock. At almost the same instant, Tate sighted a column of smoke on beyond.

Hauling the buggy to an instant halt, he hurried to the rear of it and untied his horse. He mounted and kicked the horse into a lope.

Prudence urged the willing buggy horse along after him as fast as the horse would go. As Tate passed the Hendricks' house, she saw Olaf Hendricks mount barebacked and ride after him, a rifle in his hand.

The column of smoke was growing thicker now, rising straight up in the still morning air. It was coming from the Bronson homestead. Silently Prudence began to pray that none of the Bronsons had been hurt or killed.

Chapter 13

Shawcroft, Hardesty, and Montoya watched the fire from a knoll about half a mile from the Bronson house. They saw Sheriff Tate galloping along the road toward it and saw Hendricks coming along behind, more slowly because he was riding a work horse barebacked.

Fortunately for Elias Bronson and his wife, they had been on their way to town when the cattlemen came. Now Shawcroft growled, "Maybe that'll teach the damn sodbusters that we're not going to quit even if we didn't catch them home."

Hardesty took his wide-brimmed cavalry hat off and wiped his forehead. "I still think we ought to've hit Hendricks. He's the one holding the rest of them together. And he was the first to crack after we burned Dunson out. I figure he'll crack this time, too."

Shawcroft saw a buggy dusting along the

road between the Hendricks and Bronson homesteads. He turned his head to glance at Montoya. "Go on back home. We're all done here."

Montoya seemed glad enough to go. He headed his horse across country toward Shawcroft's ranch.

Hardesty asked, "What did you do that for?"

"Send him home? See that buggy? The Dunson woman is driving it."

"You mean you think we ought to get rid of her?"

"Why not, if we get the chance? She's the one that's keeping this whole thing going. Without her, the settlers will fold up and leave."

"But a woman. . . ."

"That didn't bother you the night we hanged Sam Dunson. It didn't keep you from riding your horse into her and slamming her against the house."

"That was different. She had a gun on us."

"You think she ain't got a gun on us now? Because of her, every damned homesteader in the country has moved back onto his place. We're right back where we were before we got rid of her husband and burned her house."

"The sheriff's down there. So is Hendricks."

Shawcroft stared at him patiently. "Use your head. What will Tate do when he finds out there's no chance of saving anything?"

"Look around for the trail of whoever burned the place."

"Right. And he'll follow it."

"Then we'd better get the hell out of here."

"Right. We make trail away from here, then double back. By that time, Hendricks ought to've gone home and Mrs. Dunson will be following. Only she'll be a mile or so behind."

"It won't work."

"Maybe not, but it's worth a try." Shawcroft turned his horse and spurred him into a lope. Hardesty followed about a dozen yards behind.

Shawcroft followed Montoya's trail for a couple of miles. Then he swerved sharply to the left down into a long, sandy draw that led back toward the Bronson place. He kept his horse at a steady lope, secure in the knowledge that this draw was not visible to anyone following the trail they had made a few minutes before. Shawcroft was aware that they were cutting this pretty close, but he had already made up his mind that if Tate caught up with them they'd simply get rid of Tate. They'd gone too far to get squeamish now.

A quarter-mile short of the Bronson place, Shawcroft reined his horse up a shallow slope to a point from which he could see. Both house and barn were completely consumed, and were now only piles of smoldering rubble. Hendricks had disappeared, as had Sheriff Tate. Prudence Dunson was about a quarter-mile down the road, the buggy horse plodding along at a walk.

Shawcroft looked at Hardesty. "Couldn't be better. Let's get it over with."

Hardesty glanced worriedly in the direction Tate had gone, his hesitation based on concern for his own safety rather than on scruples over what they were about to do. Shawcroft said impatiently, "Come on. We haven't got all day."

Hardesty nodded. He followed Shawcroft toward the lone buggy traveling so slowly along the road.

Tate rode hard for about fifteen minutes. The trail he was following was plain, made by three horses. Judging by the time the Bronson buildings had taken to burn, he knew the trail could not be more than an hour old, and was probably considerably less than that.

He topped a slight rise from which he was able to see several miles ahead. He was surprised to see a single rider a couple of miles away. He drew his horse to a halt, frowning now with puzzlement. Three riders had made this trail not long ago but only one was now ahead of him. Which meant the other two had left him and gone some other way.

In his own mind he was sure the three riders had been Shawcroft, Hardesty, and Montoya. The one ahead was probably Montoya. Now he asked himself why Shawcroft and Hardesty had gone off by themselves and where they could have gone.

The answer to that wasn't difficult to come by, and suddenly Tate remembered the place where all three had apparently stopped to look back. He had guessed at the time that they had only wanted to be sure the fire was burning well, but now was forced to the uneasy conclusion that they had watched his arrival, that of Hendricks, and that of Prudence Dunson shortly afterward.

Tate hesitated no longer. He whirled his

147

horse and dug the animal's sides with his heels. He had left Bronson's following this trail. Hendricks had probably gone back home. Which meant Prudence Dunson was probably alone, driving her buggy back toward the Hendricks place. What better opportunity did Shawcroft and Hardesty need if they really wanted Prudence Dunson dead?

Digging in his heels, slashing his horse's rump with the ends of the reins, Tate thundered back toward the Bronson place. At the top of the knoll from which the three men had earlier watched the place, he glimpsed Prudence Dunson's buggy moving slowly along the road, and he saw the two horsemen riding to intercept.

Prudence obviously had not seen them yet. Nor would she, unless she happened to look back. Tate drummed heels frantically against his horse's sides, wishing he had spurs. He lashed the horse's rump with the ends of the reins.

Down off the knoll he thundered, raising a plume of dust behind. Even as he did, he could see it was no use. Shawcroft and Hardesty were going to reach the buggy a long time before he would be able to reach them. They'd kill Prudence and then would turn on him. Even if he managed to kill or capture them both it would be too late for Prudence Dunson.

A man doesn't think too well in the kind of situation in which Tate found himself. He feels. Right now he felt that if Prudence Dunson died it would be intolerable for him. Recently widowed she might be. But that fact didn't shut off what Tate felt for her.

Almost without thinking, he yanked his rifle from its saddle boot. He levered in a shell, pointed it loosely toward the galloping pair, and fired it. He levered in another shell and fired a second time. If he let them know he was here, they might change their plans.

The pair swung around in their saddles and looked at him. Their faces were white blurs through the dust raised by their galloping horses' hoofs. Tate fired again, levered in another shell, and fired again. Holding reins and rifle in his left hand, he fumbled for cartridges with which to reload.

But it wasn't necessary. The pair ahead of him abandoned their pursuit of Prudence Dunson's buggy. They swerved to the right and headed back in the direction they had originally been traveling.

Tate hesitated. He supposed he ought to

go after them. He also knew how foolish it would be. They were two and he was only one. They were desperate and wouldn't hesitate to kill him if they could.

Prudence had drawn her buggy to a halt. He could see her white face peering after the departing pair. He thundered up to the buggy and yanked his plunging horse to a halt. "Could you tell who they were?"

Her voice was thin and scared. "Shawcroft and Hardesty. They were going to kill me, weren't they?"

"That's what they had in mind." He was suddenly furious with her. "Damn it, how long are you going to . . . !" His voice trailed off. She hadn't done anything to be scolded for. He said, "I'll ride with you as far as Olaf's house."

She studied him a moment, seeing, he thought, a lot more than he wanted her to see. With her face slightly pinker than it had been before, she picked up the reins and slapped the buggy horse's back with them.

Tate fell in behind. Now that it was over, he felt weak and shaky. He gripped the horse with his knees to keep them from trembling. If he hadn't gotten suspicious and turned back, if he hadn't seen Montoya ahead of him, alone. . . .

One thing he knew for sure. Things were different now. He could arrest Shawcroft, Hardesty, and Montoya for burning Bronson's house and barn. Maybe that would put an end to the violence that had so suddenly come to the countryside. More important, maybe then Prudence Dunson would be safe.

Montoya knew when Shawcroft sent him home alone what they were going to do. He also knew he couldn't stop them. Not by himself. And by the time he got some help it was going to be too late. Prudence Dunson would be dead.

Montoya hadn't particularly liked his part in the attack on Sam Dunson's homestead. Until the last minute he hadn't even known the four cowmen meant to kill the man. He'd thought they meant to drag him, or pretend to string him up, and thus scare him enough to make him leave the land.

Montoya had the same feeling about the land the cowmen did. That wasn't surprising, considering he had worked for Shawcroft nearly a dozen years. He knew, as Shawcroft did, that the coming of settlers meant the end of open range. No man had enough money to own all the land he needed to keep his herds. Which left cattlemen with only one alternative. Drive the settlers away. Drive them away before they could put down roots, before there were enough of them to exert any political clout.

But killing women . . . Montoya wanted no part of that. He changed direction slightly and headed straight for town. When the sheriff came back, he was going to tell him everything. About the attack on the Dunson ranch. About the death of McAndrews, too.

Maybe then the whole thing would stop. He kicked his horse into a trot, grinning shakily to himself. Maybe also, he thought wryly, he could stay alive. The attack on Dunson's homestead had been made by seven men. Already four of them were dead. That was enough to make the most unsuperstitious of men wonder at what was happening.

Looking back, he saw a lone horseman following him. He saw the horseman stop, then turn and go back in the direction from which he had come, galloping. The distance had been too great for recognition but the lone horseman had probably been Sheriff Tate.

Montoya kept going. When he reached town, he went to the saloon, got down, and tied.

At this time of day, the saloon was practically deserted. Montoya asked for a bottle and a glass and took it to a table in the corner. He poured himself a good, stiff drink. He didn't think Shawcroft and Hardesty would come to town after they killed Prudence Dunson but it was a possibility. He sat in such a way that he could keep his eyes on the door.

He didn't know why he was so afraid, but he was. They had no reason to believe he was going to the sheriff and would spill the beans. But then, look what had happened to McAndrews. McAndrews had tried to balk and now McAndrews was dead.

Montoya took another drink. He seldom drank and had a low tolerance for alcohol. His head began to spin.

He pushed the bottle away from him. The door was blurring now and he was seeing double. He put his head down on the table.

The world began to spin. Montoya raised his head again. He took another drink and put his head down a second time.

This time he slept. When he awakened, it was dusk outside. With his head pounding, he got up and staggered to the door.

The bartender called to him, and he swerved to the bar, slamming a dollar down on it. Without waiting for change, he headed for the door again. The sheriff ought to be back in town by now. The compulsion to unburden his soul was suddenly overpowering. He headed down the street toward the jail.

Chapter 14

Sheriff Tate sat with his feet upon his desk. It was turning dark but he had not yet lighted a lamp.

He had left Prudence Dunson with the Hendricks family, feeling she would be as safe there as anywhere. There was no use trying to go after Shawcroft and Hardesty tonight. Tomorrow he would raise a posse. The two cowmen weren't going to run. Used to power and influence, they both would think they could buy or bluff their way out of this as they had out of other things in the past.

He glanced up as Montoya came in the door, then put his feet down on the floor and snatched out his gun. Harshly he asked, "What the hell do *you* want?"

Montoya stopped just inside the door, trying to penetrate the gloom with his glance. Tate, seeing he was harmless, put his gun away. He got up, struck a match, and lighted the lamp on his desk. Montoya stumbled to a chair facing the desk and sank into it. He peered at the sheriff owlishly. "I come to confess."

Tate said, "All right. Go ahead."

Montoya said, "I was with 'em when they hanged Sam Dunson but I ain't going to be part of killin' women. No sir, not me."

This was what Tate had been hoping for all along — one of the participants confessing all. He said, "All right. You sober enough to know what you're saying?"

"I ain't had but three drinks. I went to sleep an' I just woke up."

"You know what you're doing? You know you'll go to jail along with the rest of them?"

"Most of them are dead. I will be too if I don't stop it now."

"All right. Tell me about it."

"There was seven of us. I guess you know who they were."

"You tell me."

"Shawcroft and me. Hardesty and Mc-Andrews. Laughton and Finney. And Gibbs."

"All right, go on."

"Dunson didn't kill the steer they accused him of killing. I did. I skinned it out and we took the hide over there. I thought they was just going to throw a scare into him. I didn't know they was going to hang him and hurt his wife."

"Who did hurt her?"

"Hardesty. She had a gun and it looked like she was going to use it so Hardesty slammed his horse into her. Then they hanged Dunson and burned the house and barn."

"You'll swear to this in court?"

Montoya nodded dumbly.

"And you know you'll go to jail?"

Again Montoya nodded.

Tate said, "All right. Come on out back and I'll lock you in."

Montoya followed him back to one of the cells. Tate didn't light the lamp in the corridor, knowing Montoya would be safer in the dark. They couldn't kill him if they couldn't see him. Montoya asked almost timidly, "Did they kill her?"

Tate said, "No. I got there in time to scare them off." He locked the cell door. He went back into the office, blew out the lamp, and stepped into the street, locking the door behind him. With what he had now he could put both Shawcroft and Hardesty in prison for twenty years. If they didn't hang.

It was over. Or it would be over as soon as he had the pair in jail. In the meantime, Montoya's life was in deadly jeopardy.

There was a good chance Shawcroft and Hardesty had gone home and would stay there. But there was also a chance that when Shawcroft discovered Montoya wasn't at the ranch, he'd guess where he had gone and what he had done.

Tate went first to Eric Larsen's place. Larsen was a big, raw-boned, light-haired man who ran the town blacksmith shop. Eric answered his knock and Tate told him swiftly what the problem was. Finished, he said, "Get your shotgun, load it, and go down to the jail. Guard the front door until I get back."

He hurried away. Larsen would keep Montoya safe until he could get back with a couple more men. Tate wasn't fool enough to think he could guard Montoya against Shawcroft and Hardesty by himself. Between them, they had at least twenty men.

He went to Eli Pollock's next, and sent Pollock to join Larsen at the jail. Steve Gamble was the third man on his list, and he waited for Gamble to get his gun and then returned to the jail with him.

He outlined the problem swiftly. "Shawcroft's foreman, Montoya, has confessed to hanging Sam Dunson and burning his place. He's implicated Shawcroft and Hardesty, and I figure when Shawcroft finds out he's missing, he may guess that he's spilled the beans. They may try and kill him and I want to be ready for them if they do. Larsen, you take the alley. Pollock, you take the north side of the jail, and, Steve, you take the south. Stay in the shadows. Sit down if you want, but don't go to sleep. If they come, give 'em a warning, and if they don't skeedaddle, blast away."

He watched the three men move away and disappear into the darkness. Satisfied that he had done all he could, he unlocked the jail and went inside. He slammed home the bolt, crossed the room, and sat down. He laid his revolver on the desk in front of him. He didn't light the lamp.

It was going to be a long night, he knew. Likely nothing would happen but he didn't dare count on it.

As soon as Shawcroft was sure Sheriff Tate wasn't following, he pulled his lathered, galloping horse to a walk. Hardesty drew alongside of him. He looked at Shawcroft with eyes that betrayed his fear.

"He recognized us. The son-of-a-bitch knew who we were."

Shawcroft stared at him disgustedly. "Are you sure you were in the war?"

"What the hell do you mean by that?"

"I mean as gutless as you are, you'd have turned tail the first time you heard a gun go off."

The statement was so blunt, so utterly contemptuous, that for the moment Hardesty didn't have anything to say. His face turned dark, his eyes flashed his anger, but he finally managed to get out, "God damn you, you can't talk that way to me!"

"Who's to stop me? You?"

The two stood staring at each other for what seemed an interminable length of time. It was Hardesty who looked away. But before he did, he gave Shawcroft a look that was utterly wild and murderous. A proud and pompous man, his pride had been destroyed. His own image of himself, gilded by the trappings of the war, had been wrecked and lay in rubble at his feet. Shawcroft grunted, "Go on home."

"What are you going to do?"

"I'll think of something."

"Like what?"

"So far all Tate has got is a glimpse of us from a quarter-mile away. He can't swear

160

in court that it was us."

"What about that woman?"

"Nobody will believe her. She's accused us before and this time it'll look like she's just trying to make the other accusation stick."

"What if he trails us?"

Shawcroft frowned. He hesitated several moments and then he said, "All right. Maybe we'd better ride on into town. He can't trail us through the streets."

He kicked his horse into motion. Hardesty followed, sitting straight in the saddle, trying unconsciously to salvage the shreds of his pride. Shawcroft bore right until he struck Montoya's trail and then followed it.

He'd told Montoya to go home. But as he rode, it became increasingly evident that Montoya wasn't going there. He was headed for town instead. They were still a mile from town when Hardesty said, "I thought you told Montoya to go home."

"I did but it don't look like he went."

"You got any idea why?"

"Maybe he just wanted a drink." But Shawcroft didn't think that was the reason Montoya had come to town. He had the uneasy feeling Montoya might have come to spill the beans. The man had been acting strange since McAndrews had been shot.

Shawcroft drew his horse to a halt in front of the saloon. Montoya's horse was standing tied at the rail. He said, "He just wanted a drink." He dismounted and stuck his head into the saloon. Montoya was sitting at a table, his head down, asleep.

Disgustedly Shawcroft said, "The damn fool never could drink." He thought about waking Montoya and accompanying him home, then decided against it. He didn't feel up to nursemaiding a drunk right now.

Remounting, he looked at Hardesty. "I figure it's safe for you to go home."

Hardesty's face flushed slightly and his eyes narrowed dangerously. Shawcroft wondered if he hadn't pushed the man unnecessarily. Hardesty might not be what he thought he was but that didn't mean he wasn't dangerous.

Together, the two rode down the street and out of town.

Shawcroft arrived home about dusk. He didn't know exactly why he was uneasy but he was. He tried to put his finger on it and decided maybe it was because he thought Tate could identify the hoofprints of the horse he had ridden this afternoon.

Having decided that, he went out and got the blacksmith from the bunkhouse and told him to shoe the horse. Relieved, he returned to the house while the blacksmith led the horse into the blacksmith shop and began to heat up the forge.

But his uneasiness didn't disappear. He examined his own feelings and decided Montoya was behind his uneasiness. He'd told Montoya to go home and ordinarily Montoya would have obeyed. It was the fact that he had not, added to his drinking, which was most unusual, that so troubled him.

When darkness came, he hurried out of the house again. He went to the corral, caught himself a horse, and saddled up. He rode out again, heading toward town.

He stopped at Hardesty's. Hardesty, as uneasy as he was, seemed most willing to return to town. The two men maintained a steady trot all the way, arriving a little after eight.

Montoya's horse was no longer tied in front of the saloon. Shawcroft handed the reins of his horse to Hardesty and peered inside. Montoya wasn't there. He looked at the bartender. "What time did Montoya leave?"

"About dusk. Didn't he come home?"

"Doesn't seem so. He drink enough to've passed out someplace?"

"He only had three drinks."

Shawcroft withdrew. He took the reins from Hardesty and mounted. He said, "He left about dusk. And we didn't pass him on the road. Which means he must still be in town."

"You think he went to Tate?"

"I think he might. Let's ride past the jail. Maybe we can see into the window on the side."

He led the way down the street and into the vacant lot beside the jail. A voice called out, "That's far enough, gents. Go on back to the street and everything will be all right."

The voice confirmed Shawcroft's fears. Montoya had cracked. He'd gone to the sheriff and had confessed.

Shawcroft rode back to the street. Hardesty, right behind him, said, "Tate's sure as hell got him in jail."

"Looks like it."

"Now what?" Hardesty's voice was thin.

Shawcroft felt a savage compulsion to needle him. "What would Colonel Hardesty have done during the war?"

"God damn you . . . !"

Shawcroft controlled himself with difficulty. Needling Hardesty wasn't going to help the mess that they were in. He said, "Sorry."

He rode down the street so that they'd be out of sight of the jail. At the end of it he halted. "We've got to get that son-of-a-bitch."

"How? Tate's got guards around the jail. We only saw one but I'll bet he's got at least two more."

Shawcroft frowned. "There ought to be some way of drawing them away."

"I don't know what it would be. We could start shooting but I doubt if it would work."

"How about fire? Nobody ignores a fire."

"No, they don't."

"There's an old house at the upper end of town. Nobody's living in it. There'll be no way anybody downtown can tell what's burning until they're halfway there."

Shawcroft led the way by a circuitous route to the upper end of town. They'd have to move fast after the fire bell began to ring. They'd only have a few minutes to break into the jail and kill Montoya. He might have talked to the sheriff but the word of a dead man wasn't going to hold up very well in court.

Chapter 15

The door of the vacant house stood open. Shawcroft and Hardesty left their horses tied to the sagging fence and went up the gravel path. Inside, Shawcroft lighted a match and peered around. There was a pile of dry leaves, papers, and trash in one corner. Shawcroft tossed the match into it.

By the light of the growing blaze, he and Hardesty went around the room gathering up broken boards, which they laid carefully on the fire. Made uneasy by the light, they nevertheless stayed until the blaze was several feet high, until it had caught the wall. Then they hurried out.

The two horses were pulling back against their tied reins, having smelled the smoke and seen the blaze. Their ears were laid back, their eyes rolling with fear. Shawcroft and Hardesty mounted and returned to the center of town. It would be a while before anyone noticed the fire. Time enough to get set, to be ready when Tate and the guards left the jail.

In front of the saloon, Shawcroft halted his horse. He dismounted and tied, saying, "Stay on your horse. I'll go in the front as soon as Tate goes out. I'll get some light back where Montoya is and you shoot him through the window."

"What about you?" Hardesty asked suspiciously. "What are you going to be doing?"

Shawcroft stared at him disgustedly. "I'm goin' to get him in a crossfire to be sure we kill him."

Hardesty grumbled something Shawcroft didn't hear. Shawcroft watched him ride away. Hardesty positioned himself in a vacant lot across from the jail, hard against a building wall where he would be invisible.

Shawcroft stared toward the upper end of town, looking for the light of the fire. He wondered briefly if it had died out, then put that thought out of his mind. It hadn't died out. It just hadn't grown large enough to be easily seen as yet.

Five minutes passed and finally Shawcroft saw a reddish glow against the sky. Another two or three minutes passed before he heard faint, shouting voices from the same direction.

The shouting grew louder as those who had seen the fire raced toward the center of town. Shawcroft realized how tense he was. He'd be glad when this was all over with, he thought. He'd be glad when Montoya was dead. He didn't think Hardesty would come apart the way Montoya had. And with both their crews, they ought to be able to get rid of Prudence Dunson and once more drive the settlers off the land. They could still do that if they were ruthless and determined enough.

The fire bell began to ring. The saloon erupted men and the door of the jail opened. Tate stood framed in it. He glanced uptown toward the blaze that now was a huge red glow in the sky. Closing the door behind him, he started up the street.

He stopped suddenly, hesitated, then returned to the jail and locked the door. After that he ran up the street and disappeared. Men came from both sides of the jail, two from one side, one from the other. They also disappeared in the direction of the fire.

Shawcroft wasted no time, but crossed the street at a run. He raised a foot and kicked the side of the door. It didn't give, so he kicked again. This time the doorjamb splintered and the door flew open.

Shawcroft went in, his revolver in his hand. He crossed the room, snatching up a lamp as he went. Carrying it in his left hand, he went into the corridor between the cells.

Montoya was standing on his bunk, looking out the window and trying to see what all the excitement was about. He turned his head when he heard the door.

His eyes widened with fear. He opened his mouth to say something, then closed it without doing so. His eyes fixed themselves on Shawcroft's gun, their expression plainly saying he knew it was no use to beg. He was going to die and there was nothing on earth he could do about it.

Shawcroft didn't fire. He was waiting for Hardesty to appear at the window. Like Hardesty, he didn't want to be the only one guilty in Montoya's death.

Hardesty appeared and poked his gun between the bars. Montoya glanced toward him, his face as gray as a winter sky.

Shawcroft fired first. Montoya's body twitched. Hardesty fired. His slug, for some reason, slammed Montoya back against the stone cell wall. He hung there for an instant, as if something was supporting him.

Shawcroft fired again, and his second shot was followed closely by a second from

Hardesty. His shirt front a welter of blood, Montoya collapsed.

He was dead. Shawcroft knew that without going into the cell. He holstered his smoking gun, backed into the sheriff's office, and put the lamp down on the desk. He hurried out into the street, across it, and back to the saloon where his horse was tied. He mounted and headed through a vacant lot to the alley.

The fire bell was still ringing. The distant sounds of shouting mingled with that sound and with the fire's roar. Reddish light cast shadows on the ground even this far away.

Hardesty joined Shawcroft and the two headed out of town. Now, at least, nobody was going to talk. All that remained was getting rid of the Dunson woman. When that was done, the settlers would be terrified enough to leave.

Tate knew the instant he saw the fire that he had been duped. Being consumed was an old vacant house that should have been torn down years ago. Shawcroft and Hardesty had set the blaze for the sole purpose of drawing him and the guards he had posted away from the jail.

He whirled immediately and sprinted

back toward the jail, knowing even as he did that he was going to be too late. Montoya would be dead when he arrived, and there would be no one to testify against Shawcroft and Hardesty.

Savagely and helplessly he cursed his own stupidity. He met the guards running toward him from the jail and he roared, "It's a trick! Get back to the jail!"

They turned and followed him. The jail door was standing open when he reached it and he knew he was too late. Gun in hand, he burst inside and ran to the cell block at the rear. That door also stood open.

The cells were dark so he returned and got the lamp. By its light he saw Montoya slumped against the stone cell wall, his chest red with blood.

Swiftly, Tate unlocked the cell. He went in and knelt beside Montoya. There was no pulse.

He beckoned one of the three he had positioned outside as guards. Together the two lifted Montoya and laid him on the bunk. Tate drew the blanket up over his face.

Returning to the office, he felt a small chill run along his spine. It was eerie, the things that were happening. Prudence Dunson, a lone, weak, nearly helpless woman had sworn vengeance against the seven men who had killed her husband. Now a week later five of those seven men were dead.

Maybe even more important, her apparent success had encouraged the settlers to return to their homes. Even the burning of Bronson's place hadn't frightened them away again.

Tate closed the door that separated the office and the cells. He looked at the three men. "You three can go on home. There's nothing to keep you here any more."

They looked at him strangely, he thought, but none of them said anything. They went out, one trying to close the door but failing because of the splintered jamb.

Tate sat down at his desk. He'd have to get Montoya's body taken care of, he thought. He'd have to question everybody he could find to see if they'd seen anybody entering or leaving the jail.

His mind kept going back to the five dead men. Five, all killed in a matter of days. Again that small chill stirred in Tate's spine.

Finally he got up and crossed the street to the saloon. Men were beginning to straggle back to it. The glow in the sky was gone. Tate heard one man say, ". . . nothin'

172

we could do. We finally decided to just let it burn."

Tate went into the saloon. He stood with his back to the bar and shouted, "Anybody see anyone go into the jail in the last twenty minutes or so?"

Nobody had. Tate really hadn't expected anything different. When there was a fire nobody paid any attention to anything else. Everybody knew that fire could spread and destroy a whole town in a frighteningly short time if it wasn't controlled.

A man asked, "What happened, sheriff?"

"Somebody set that fire. While everybody was up there they broke into the jail and killed Montoya."

"Shawcroft and Hardesty?"

"Sure," Tate said bitterly. "But try proving it in court." He remembered that he had to do something about Montoya's body. He said, "Go see if Rufus is home. Tell him to get a couple of men and pick Montoya up."

The man went out. Tate ordered a bottle and a glass. He poured the glass half full and drank it. He made a face and pushed the bottle away from him.

He left a dime on the bar, went out, and walked back to the jail. Rufus was there supervising the removal of Montoya's body.

Tate figured he was going to say something about how good business was and he did.

Tate stared sourly after the three men carrying Montoya on a stretcher. He thought about Prudence Dunson and he suddenly began worrying about where Shawcroft and Hardesty might have gone after leaving here.

Even though it was dark, and late, he crossed to the livery stable and, in the darkness, caught and saddled a horse. He mounted and rode out, heading toward Olaf Hendricks' place. Reluctantly he admitted to himself that his concern for Prudence Dunson's safety was more than official concern. He was in love with her. He would have to wait a decent interval, probably a year. But as soon as that interval had passed, he intended to ask her to marry him.

Chapter 16

Shawcroft and Hardesty were no more than half a dozen miles out of town when Shawcroft suddenly hauled his horse to a halt. Hardesty asked, "What's the matter with you?"

"That damned Dunson woman."

"What about her?"

"She swore she'd get even with us for killing her husband. She said if the law couldn't take care of it, she was going to."

"So what?"

"She's damned near done it. Montoya was the fifth."

"She didn't kill Montoya. We did."

"Sure. But why?" Shawcroft asked patiently.

"So he wouldn't talk."

"Right. So he wouldn't talk about the night we hanged Sam Dunson. It all ties together. Every one of the five that died either was killed by her or died because of what we did that night. She scared Gibbs into falling down his own well. She shot Laughton. She stampeded that herd of cattle and killed Finney doing it. We killed McAndrews because he balked and Montoya because he'd spilled the beans. But every death ties into what was done at Dunson's place."

"What are you getting at?"

"We've got to get rid of her. Before she gets rid of the two of us."

"But not now. Not right away, at least."

"I didn't say we had to do it ourselves. I said we had to get rid of her. With the way things are in this country right now, I don't want to be within fifty miles when she gets hers."

"How, then?"

"You remember that trial in Cheyenne a few months back? Where the guy was charged with killin' a twelve-year-old boy?"

"Yeah. I remember. He got off because they didn't have enough evidence."

"Well, he's still in Cheyenne, or was last time I was there. And he killed that kid. I'm sure of it. He shouldn't mind killin' a woman if he'd kill a kid."

"Good idea. Let's send for him."

"Maybe there's a better way. We don't want nothing tying either of us to him. If you take off for Cheyenne right now, you can be there by dark tomorrow if you ride all night."

Hardesty was silent, but only for an instant. Then he said, "No, you don't. If I hire him, I'm the one that will get tied to her death if he gets caught."

Shawcroft sighed. "All right. We'll both go. Will your wife wonder about it if you're gone a couple of days?"

"Not enough to stir up a fuss."

"All right then." Shawcroft turned his horse south and kicked him into a trot, wondering why he hadn't thought of this before. The death of Prudence Dunson would reaffirm what her husband's death had originally done. It would scare the living hell out of the settlers. They'd leave their land a second time and this time they would not come back.

Surprised at how relieved he felt, he admitted to himself that Prudence Dunson's success in getting rid of those she had sworn vengeance against had worried him. There was little doubt that she had been lucky. She obviously had been aided either by chance or circumstances. Or by the intervention of some supernatural force. This kind of thinking, he supposed, was at the root of his nervousness, and no amount of scoffing seemed to make it go away.

They maintained a fairly steady pace all through the night, alternately walking and trotting their horses. At sunup, they rode into the yard of an isolated ranch owned by a man both knew. He gave them breakfast, loaned them fresh horses, and promised to feed and care for theirs so they could pick them up on their way home tomorrow.

They rode out again, maintaining the same hard pace, and in late afternoon rode into Cheyenne. They stabled the horses and walked to the hotel, where they got a room.

Neither wanted it later recalled that they had been inquiring around town for Morton Frye. So Shawcroft gave a five-dollar gold piece to a seedy-looking drifter passing in front of the hotel, told him Frye's name, and told him there'd be another five when he found the man. The drifter scurried away as if afraid Shawcroft would change his mind.

It was late when the drifter and Morton Frye appeared at the hotel. Both Shawcroft and Hardesty were sitting on the wide veranda, their booted feet up on the rail. Shawcroft handed the drifter the other five. The man scurried away, heading for the nearest saloon. Frye asked suspiciously, "What do you want me for?"

Shawcroft glanced around. There were others on the veranda, all listening. He said, "It's a nice night. Why don't we take a walk?"

"All right." Frye was a slender man but a powerful one. If he had a gun, it didn't show. He was dressed in a pair of baggy woolen pants, a flannel shirt, and a vest. He wore rider's boots and had topped the outfit off with a brown derby hat. Shawcroft didn't like or trust him, but he didn't suppose liking was necessary, or even desirable.

When they had walked half a block or so he said, "We want to hire you."

"What for?"

"A killing."

"Who?"

"A woman. In a place called Broken Arrow. Know where it is?"

"I know. Who's the woman? Your wife?"

"Settler woman. As long as she's alive, the settlers aren't going to leave."

"What do I get paid?"

Shawcroft hesitated. He'd meant to offer the man a hundred dollars but he heard his own voice say, "Five hundred dollars."

"What's this woman look like and where can I find her in Broken Arrow?"

Shawcroft described Prudence Dunson to him. He said she would probably be staying out at the Hendricks place and he gave Frye directions for getting there. He emphasized that he didn't want any mistakes. He didn't want the wrong woman killed.

"I want two hundred now."

"I'll have to get it at the bank tomorrow."

"I can wait."

Shawcroft said, "We don't want to be seen meeting you."

"Alley behind the bank, then."

Shawcroft said, "One thing," as Frye started away.

The man turned. "What's that?"

"Five hundred is a lot. If you're caught, you're on your own. We don't know you."

"Fair enough. Provided I get the rest of the money."

"You'll get it."

"Nine o'clock tomorrow, then. Behind the bank." He walked away.

Hardesty said nervously, "I need a drink."

"Let's get one, then." They headed for the nearest saloon.

Hardesty asked, "You think he'll do the job?"

"Why not? Anybody can kill a woman."

"What if he gets caught and talks?"

"We deny it. Nobody can prove anything."

They reached the saloon and went inside. Shawcroft ordered a bottle and two glasses and carried them to a table. They had two drinks each, then headed for the hotel.

At nine-fifteen the following morning, Shawcroft and Hardesty met Frye in the alley behind the bank. Shawcroft drew him into an abandoned stable and counted out ten double eagles, thinking as he did that he had no guarantee Frye wouldn't just pocket the money and disappear. It was a chance he'd just have to take, he supposed.

Frye left first and Shawcroft and Hardesty waited about ten minutes before they also left. They got their horses at the stable and rode immediately out of town, heading north.

Tate pushed his horse harder than he really wanted to on his way out to the Hendricks homestead. He was worried about Prudence Dunson's safety. He was afraid that, having eliminated Montoya,

Shawcroft and Hardesty might attack Hendricks with the intention of getting rid of Prudence once and for all.

He was intensely relieved that everything seemed peaceful when he arrived. A dog began to bark as he halted in front of their little house. Hendricks himself came to the door, a shotgun in his hands. Behind him, Tate could see Hector, also carrying a gun. When Hendricks saw who it was, he said, "Get down, sheriff, and come in."

Tate dismounted and tied his horse to the wheel of a buckboard standing in front of the house. He went in, removing his hat as he did. Prudence Dunson was sitting in a chair, some mending in her lap. She looked up at him, and a tiny smile of welcome touched her mouth. He realized suddenly that he had never really seen her smile. Not that she'd had anything to smile about.

Hendricks asked, "What brings you out here at this time of night?"

"Worry about you, maybe. Montoya came in and surrendered himself today. Implicated Shawcroft and Hardesty in the attack on Mrs. Dunson's place. I figured they might try and get to him, so I posted guards around the jail." He stopped, then forced himself to go on. "They took me in like a rube. Set a fire on the edge of town, and when we all ran to it, they broke into the jail and killed Montoya. I figured, having done that, they might come out here. I'm glad they didn't."

"How long ago did all this happen?"

"Just before I left town. They had plenty of time to get here if they'd been coming." He got up. He glanced at Prudence and saw that the smile had left her lips. Her face was somber now and her eyes would not meet his.

She was thinking that she had caused yet another death in her pursuit of vengeance but this one was not her fault. He said, "Mrs. Dunson, you can't blame yourself for this."

She didn't answer him. Her expression was like a door closed in his face. He stared at her a moment, hoping she would look up but she did not. He went to the door and stepped outside.

Hendricks followed him. Tate said, "Stay on guard. They may come yet. They still haven't given up the idea of chasing you and the others off the land, and they likely figure the quickest way would be to get rid of her."

"I know. We'll be ready if they come."

"Nobody's ever ready, and they'll have

both crews with them when they do."

"We'll make a stand inside the house."

Tate nodded. He supposed that was the best he could expect. But as he rode away he promised himself that he'd ride out here and make sure everything was all right at least once a day.

Chapter 17

Morton Frye was not a professional killer. He was a petty criminal. He had lived all of his adult life by robbing helpless travelers, by breaking into unoccupied homes and untended businesses, by stealing horses and cattle whenever he thought he could get away with it.

He had killed three times during the course of his life. At fourteen, he'd killed his stepfather to keep from being beaten. He'd run away and had not been caught.

The second person had been a middle-aged woman. She had surprised him burglarizing her store and had begun to yell. He had throttled her to shut her up.

The third had been the boy. He had been paid fifty dollars to kill the youngster by a cattleman who wanted the boy's father off his range.

Now he found himself in the position of killing again for pay. And not for chicken feed this time. Five hundred dollars for a single killing. He swaggered as he walked back to the saloon where the drifter had located him. He slapped one of the double eagles down on the bar with a flourish. Two hundred in his pocket and three hundred more when the job was done. Shawcroft needn't have worried about the two hundred dollars. Frye wanted the other three hundred to go with it. He also was eager to begin building his reputation as a professional hired gun.

Consciousness of the gold he was carrying kept him from drinking very much. He left the saloon early and went to his room in a run-down hotel near the railroad tracks. With considerable inward excitement, he told himself this was the last time he'd travel second-class. From now on it would be the best hotels, the best restaurants.

He turned in and was up at dawn, dressed carefully, and shaved. He checked out of the hotel and went to the livery stable.

For a hundred dollars he was able to buy himself a good saddle horse and a saddle that, while not new, was in good condition and looked respectable. Wondering if he hadn't bitten off more than he could chew, he rode out, heading north toward Broken Arrow and the job he had contracted to do.

Sheriff Jason Tate saw him ride into Broken Arrow. He stared curiously for a moment, wondering if he had ever seen this particular stranger before. He got up, walked to the door, and looked more closely at the man. The derby hat was unusual enough to arouse his curiosity.

It also rang a bell in his memory. Frowning, he went back to his desk. He rummaged through a pile of old newspapers in the bottom drawer of his desk. Halfway through he found what he had been looking for.

It was the newcomer's picture that stared back at him from the front page of the Cheyenne paper. The caption said, "Morton Frye. Acquitted of the murder of twelve-year-old Casey Brown." A brief story followed. The witness against Frye had suddenly disappeared, leaving the prosecution with no case.

Tate put the papers back. He went to the door again. Frye's horse stood tied to the rail in front of the hotel.

Tate had a probing mind. Another question he had been asking himself — "Where had Shawcroft and Hardesty been for the last four days?" — and "What was Frye doing in Broken Arrow?" suddenly came together and provided an answer to both questions. Shawcroft and Hardesty had been in Cheyenne. Frye was here at their behest, either to intimidate the settlers by gunning down one of them or to murder Prudence Dunson, with the same result.

Having reached this conclusion, however tentatively, Tate headed for the hotel. Frye was at the desk, signing the register. Tate came up beside him. "Morton Frye, isn't it?"

The man turned. His eyes were pale blue. There was a certain defiant bravado in his face. "What if I am?"

"Mind telling me what your business in Broken Arrow is?"

"I don't have to tell you that."

"Guess you don't. I don't have to tell you why I'm ordering you to leave, either."

"Are you ordering me to leave?"

"Yes. You've got forty-eight hours." He wished as soon as it was out that he had said twenty-four.

Frye's expression didn't change, yet Tate knew somehow that forty-eight hours was all Frye thought he was going to need. Frye said, "I'll be gone, sheriff."

"See that you are." Tate turned and left

the hotel without looking back.

Walking back to the jail, he cursed soundlessly to himself. Now he'd have to keep an eye on Frye. He'd have to follow him everywhere he went. Still, he thought, maybe that was better anyway. If he could catch Frye in the act of trying to kill one of the settlers, or Prudence Dunson, maybe he could get him to implicate the pair that had hired him. Frye didn't look as if he could stand much pressure. He wasn't the professional killer type. He was more like a petty criminal, a sneak thief who would avoid confrontations at any cost.

Tate went into the jail and sat down, but he could not sit still. What if Frye sneaked out the back door of the hotel? What if he managed to get out to Hendricks' without his, Tate's, knowing it?

He got up and began to pace uneasily back and forth. Neither Shawcroft nor Hardesty would hire a killer for anyone but Prudence Dunson, he thought. If they'd wanted Hendricks dead they'd have done it themselves. He didn't need to hang around town trying to keep an eye on Frye. What he should do was ride out to the Hendricks place and be waiting for Frye when he arrived.

The decision made him feel a lot easier

in his mind. He went out and hurried to the livery stable. He got his horse and left by the back door of the stable so that Frye, if he happened to be watching, wouldn't see him leave.

He reached Hendricks' at noon, in time to be invited for dinner. He sat down at the table across from Prudence Dunson, pleased to see a small smile of welcome on her mouth.

He'd given Frye forty-eight hours and the man had seemed satisfied with that much time. So he'd just stay here, under one pretext or another, until Frye had made his move.

When dinner was finished, Tate, Hendricks, and Hector went outside. Tate fired up his pipe and Hendricks followed suit. The three squatted comfortably in the shade of a small shed that served as a barn. There was silence between them for a while. Finally Hendricks asked, "What are you doing out here, Tate?"

"Just riding by."

"When are you going back?"

Tate shrugged.

Again there was silence, broken finally by Hendricks. "Why don't you tell me why you're really here? You didn't just happen to be passing by."

Tate grinned faintly. "All right. Shaw-croft and Hardesty have been missing for the last four days. And suddenly, today, that killer shows up from Cheyenne."

"Which killer?"

"Morton Frye. The one who killed that boy."

"The one they turned loose because the witness disappeared?"

"Uh-huh."

"Did you talk to him?"

"Yep. He wouldn't say why he was here so I gave him forty-eight hours to leave. It didn't seem to upset him much so I gathered forty-eight hours was enough for what he meant to do."

"And you figure that's to get rid of Mrs. Dunson?"

"That's what I think."

Hendricks whistled. "You going to stay here until he shows up?"

"If you don't mind."

"Hell, I don't mind. What about the women? You want to keep it from them?"

"I think so. No use scaring them. I could be wrong."

"If you're wrong, you'll be out here while somebody's getting killed in town."

"I guess that's a chance I'll have to take."

"What kind of story can you come up

with to explain you being here?"

"Maybe no story at all. Maybe I can just hide out in the shed."

"For two days? It isn't possible. It wouldn't fool them one damn bit."

"Then I guess they'll have to know."

"Might be better if they did. That way they can be on guard." He peered closely at Tate. "You don't give Prudence Dunson enough credit, Tate. She's got a lot of sand. So has my wife, for that matter. Neither one of them has to be shielded from the realities of life."

"Maybe not."

Still studying Tate closely, Hendricks said, "Prudence Dunson is some woman, isn't she? Pretty. And young. And strong. When she gets through grieving for her husband, she's going to make somebody a damn fine wife."

Tate knew the blood had crept up into his face. He couldn't help himself. Because those thoughts were exactly the same as the ones he'd been having recently. Mercifully, Hendricks looked away and dropped the subject when he saw the effect of his remark. He said, "Come on in the house. We'll tell them what's going on."

The two women took the story without flinching. Both had lived with the threat of attack so long that now it was almost a relief to know the attack was imminent. It was decided that Tate would conceal himself in the shed. His horse would be turned into the corral.

Hendricks and Hector went out to where they had been working on a fence. The women did a wash. In late afternoon, Prudence came out and began to hang it on the line.

Because of the way the shed faced, and because it had only one window, Tate didn't see Frye until he was a hundred yards from Prudence. Frye had come up the draw behind the house, keeping himself concealed until he was a couple of hundred yards away.

Behind Frye, Tate saw Hendricks hurrying toward the house. Tate waited, rifle leveled and resting on the door jamb. He knew he was taking a chance with Prudence Dunson's life, but he had to wait until Frye actually drew his gun. Frye had to be caught in the act or he'd simply say he had been lost, or passing through, and would get away with it.

Prudence glanced up now and saw Tate in the doorway of the shed. Frye, coming toward her from the side of the little building, still hadn't looked toward Tate, being too intent on his victim.

Fifty feet from Prudence, Frye swung from his horse. Suddenly, he called, "Mrs. Dunson?"

She raised her head. Frye drew his gun.

Tate, his sights steady on Frye's chest, called, "Don't! I've got a gun on you."

For an instant, Frye was motionless, his gun half raised. Tate supposed Frye had depended on surprise, but he had behaved in an incredibly stupid way. He hadn't checked to see if anyone else was here. He'd seen Hendricks and Hector working in the field and he'd simply assumed the women were alone.

Frye turned his head and looked at Tate in the doorway of the shed. Then he reluctantly let the gun slip from his fingers and fall to the ground.

Tate stepped from the shed. He said, "Go in the house, Mrs. Dunson. I'll take care of him."

Prudence, her face scared, fled to the house. Tate still could not believe this was all there was. Could Frye really be as stupid as he seemed?

Tate said, "You're under arrest for attempted murder. Might go easier with you if you tell who hired you." He kept looking past Frye, half expecting to see Shawcroft and Hardesty behind him in the draw.

Frye didn't speak.

Tate said, "All I've got to do is take a ride to Cheyenne. Somebody will have seen you with them."

"Then you know who they were."

"I know."

"What if I do tell you?"

Tate said, "You haven't killed anybody. You didn't even fire your gun."

Frye's pale blue eyes didn't look dangerous. They just looked scared. He wasn't the hardened professional killer he fancied himself. He was only a petty thief, who could kill when cornered but who had neither the brains nor the raw courage to make a career of it. He cleared his throat. "I don't know their names."

"Describe them, then."

Frye did. He described Shawcroft and Hardesty. Tate said, "All right. Get your horse and we'll go back to town."

Hendricks and Hector now came hurrying up to them. Hendricks got Tate's horse and saddled him. Tate rode out with Frye ahead of him.

He'd had a witness against Shawcroft and Hardesty in his jail once before. He'd let himself be drawn away and Montoya had been killed. Now he had another witness against the pair. He wasn't going to lose this one. This one was going to put Shawcroft and Hardesty behind bars or get them hanged.

Chapter 18

Jason Tate locked Frye in a cell as soon as he arrived in town. It was near sundown, a hot, still afternoon. Several small boys gathered in front of the jail. When he went back out into the street, he called one of them over to him. "Know where Mr. Carr lives, son?"

"Yes sir."

"Get him for me. It's important." He dug in his pocket and gave the boy a nickel. The boy went up the street at a run.

The others looked disappointed. Tate said, "Don't look down in the mouth. I've got jobs for all of you." He sent one of the boys for Eric Larsen, another for Steve Gamble, a third for Eli Pollock. The fourth and last he sent to the parsonage to get the preacher to ring the fire bell.

The excited boys ran, forgetting in their excitement to wait for the nickel he had meant to give each of them. Tate waited.

After about five minutes the fire bell

began to ring. It was the same bell that was used on Sunday to call people to church, but when it was used as a fire bell it was rung with as fast a cadence as possible. People began streaming into the street.

Tate shouted at them and beckoned. They began moving toward him. He waited until there were thirty or forty people in the street, then shouted, "I've got a man in jail that Shawcroft and Hardesty hired to kill Mrs. Dunson. I want a posse to go with me to pick them up."

Hands went up instantly. Tate selected eight, thinking that Prudence Dunson had just about dispelled the fear and awe the two ranchers had once managed to command among the people of Broken Arrow. "Get your horses and guns. Meet back here in twenty minutes."

The men hurried away. The crowd remained, watching and listening expectantly. Tate beckoned to David Carr, the town carpenter. He said, "I want boards put up over the cell windows so nobody can see in, and I want the front door fixed. Can you do it right away?"

"Sure. I'll go get some lumber and my tools." Carr hurried away.

Tate called to Pollock, Larsen, and Gamble. "I want you three inside the jail. Don't let anything pull you away, and if anybody tries to get inside, shoot to kill. Is that understood?"

The three nodded soberly. They filed into the jail and Tate followed them. He unlocked the guns in the rack and passed out a double-barreled shotgun to each of the three. He got a box of shells from a desk drawer, checked to see that they were loaded with buckshot, then gave each man a handful of them. They broke their shotguns, loaded them, and snapped them shut.

Tate got a carbine for himself and loaded it. He stuck a handful of extra cartridges into his pants pocket.

Carr came in the door, accompanied by his fifteen-year-old son. Carr was carrying his toolbox. The boy was carrying several boards. Carr asked, "Which do you want done first, the windows or the door?"

"Windows."

Carr disappeared through the door leading to the cells, the boy following. Tate said, "As soon as he gets the window in the empty cell done, put the prisoner in there so he can do the other one."

Pollock said, "All right."

"And watch Frye. He knows his life is in danger and he'll get away if he can."

"He won't get away."

Outside, men who had been earlier selected as possemen were beginning to arrive. Tate went out. He mounted, rode to the livery stable, and got a fresh horse for himself. By the time he got back, all the members of the posse were waiting. In the empty cell Tate could hear Carr hammering.

Pollock, Gamble, and Larsen stood just outside the door. Tate gave them a final admonition. "If they come, they'll likely bring every man they've got. Don't hold back if they try forcing their way in."

"Yes sir."

Tate beckoned his posse and rode down the street. It was almost like a parade, with what seemed like everyone in town lining both sides of the street.

The sky was darkening fast. Tate held his horse at a trot for a while, then loped, then dropped back to a trot again. Stars winked out as the sky grew wholly black.

Lamps were burning in the house at Shawcroft's. Dogs began to bark as the posse rode into the yard. Mrs. Shawcroft came to the door. "Who is it?" she called nervously.

"It's Sheriff Tate, Mrs. Shawcroft. Is your husband here?"

"No, sheriff. Why? What do you want him for?"

"Do you know where he is?"

"He might be at Mr. Hardesty's."

"Thank you, ma'am."

"Sheriff? What's this all about?"

He didn't answer. There was no use getting her all upset and he didn't want to take time trying to explain everything to her. He wheeled his horse and led the posse out of the yard.

He had the feeling he wasn't going to find either Shawcroft or Hardesty tonight, but he led the posse on out to Hardesty's anyway. It was the same story there. Mrs. Hardesty didn't know where her husband was. She also tried to get Tate to say why he wanted him but Tate led the posse out of the yard without doing so.

One of the men asked disgustedly, "Now what?"

"Back to town, I guess."

"And then what?"

"I'll put a guard on Prudence Dunson and keep a guard on Frye. Maybe they'll come to us."

"What if they don't?"

"They'll show up sooner or later."

They arrived in town a little before midnight. The possemen scattered immediately. Tate went wearily to the jail.

The three men he had left guarding the jail were nervous and alert. The windows of the cells had been boarded up and Carr was working on the door. Tate asked, "Everything all right?"

"Sure."

Tate hesitated, worry growing in his mind. If Shawcroft and Hardesty hadn't come to town, then where had they gone? The answer was obvious. With a final admonition to Pollock, Larsen, and Gamble not to let anything pull them away from the jail, he went outside. He stood for a moment in the darkness, listening to the racket coming from the saloon across the street.

Decisively, then, he mounted his horse and headed for the Hendricks place. If Shawcroft and Hardesty weren't at home, and if they hadn't come to town, there was only one other place they could be.

Shawcroft and Hardesty were twenty-five miles away from the Hendricks place when Tate caught Frye. They were at Delaney's roadhouse and, besides Delaney, there were three other men present. Enough to provide them with iron-clad proof that they could not have been responsible for Prudence Dunson's death.

They had, however, stationed one of Shawcroft's crewmen along the road between Hendricks' and town, to observe. The man was supposed to let them know what happened and to notify them when Prudence Dunson's body was taken in to town.

At sundown the man arrived, riding a lathered horse. Shawcroft and Hardesty went outside as soon as they saw him and, far enough from the roadhouse so they could not be overheard, asked him what had happened.

"The son-of-a-bitch got caught," he said. "He seen Hendricks and his kid out in the field and he jumped to the conclusion the women was alone. Only they wasn't. Tate was there."

"Frye get killed?"

"No sir. Tate captured him."

Shawcroft cursed angrily. Hardesty said piously, "When you want a thing done right, do it yourself."

Shawcroft whirled on him. "Don't be so goddamn smug. You went to Cheyenne with me, remember?"

"Yeah, but Frye was your idea."

Shawcroft said snappishly, "Bickering isn't going to help." He looked at the crewman. "Go on back to the ranch. Get every man available. Meet us on the road between town and the Hendricks place."

"Yes sir." The man turned and rode away, urging the horse to lope. Hardesty stared at Shawcroft. "What you going to do?"

"You said it. If you want a thing done right, do it yourself."

For once Hardesty didn't have anything to say. They got their horses and headed back on a course that would strike the road between town and the Hendricks place. Both men knew that Prudence Dunson was first. Wiping out the Hendricks family was next. After that, they would get rid of Frye.

Tate rode hard, uncomfortably aware that Shawcroft and Hardesty could already have reached the Hendricks place. Whether they had or not depended, he supposed, on where they had been when Frye tried to kill Prudence. It also depended on whether or not they knew Frye had been caught.

But he'd warned Hendricks. He'd made Hendricks promise to fort up in the house if the cattlemen showed up. So even if Shawcroft and Hardesty were ahead of him, Hendricks, Hector, and the two women might have been able to hold them off.

No matter how he tried to reassure himself, his uneasiness did not go away. He wished he had brought a posse with him, but the men who had gone to Shawcroft's and Hardesty's with him had been tired and had dispersed. It would have taken time to round them up, time Tate did not want to lose.

He thought of Prudence Dunson as he rode. He caught himself wishing he didn't have to wait a whole year before he could start courting her, then he scoffed at his own foolishness. Maybe she wouldn't want him to start courting her, even when the year was up. Maybe he was just fooling himself.

He kicked his weary horse into a lope, held it as long as he dared, then let the horse trot again. About halfway to Hendricks', he suddenly hauled the horse to a halt. Ahead, he had heard a voice, and now, listening, he heard another one.

Silently, he reined his horse off the road. Circling, he put the horsemen he had heard against the faint light of the crescent moon. He couldn't count them but he knew there must be eight or ten at least. They were motionless, smoking and talking, apparently waiting for something or someone.

Slowly, carefully, Tate went on around them. Only when he was half a mile beyond did he put his horse back into the road. Relief was strong in him. Hendricks had not yet been attacked. But when the attack did come, there would be close to a dozen men. Hendricks couldn't hope to hold out against them. If he, his family, and Prudence Dunson didn't run, they were doomed. And Tate had a sudden, uncomfortable feeling that Hendricks would, this time, refuse to run.

Chapter 19

As Tate approached the Hendricks' house, the single, dim light showing through the kitchen window went out. Surprised that they still were up, but pleased at their vigilance, Tate rode closer. Getting edgy when he heard no sound, he called, "It's Tate!"

The light flickered alive again and the door opened. Tate dismounted, dropped his horse's reins on the ground, and went inside.

All four were awake and fully dressed. Tate said, "There's a bunch of eight or ten men a ways down the road. They seem to be waiting for something, but they could get here any time. I want the four of you to leave, right now. There's no way on earth you can stand up to that many men."

Prudence Dunson was watching him. He glanced at Hendricks. The man's jaw was set stubbornly, as he had expected it would be. He said, "You left last time, after Sam

Dunson was killed. What's so different about this time?"

"Maybe Mrs. Dunson has showed us it is possible to fight them, and to win."

"You can't win against a dozen men."

"All but two of them are hired hands."

"What's that got to do with it?"

"Their stake isn't as big. All they're protecting is a job."

Tate glanced at Mrs. Hendricks. "How about you, ma'am?"

"My husband is right. We will stay. We have had time to think this time and we are not afraid."

Tate studied her, then Hector. He said dryly, "No. You don't look it."

"All right. We're scared. But not enough to make us run again."

Tate now looked at Prudence. "And you?"

"I will also stay, Sheriff Tate."

Under his steady regard, her face flushed. He said, "You don't give a man much choice."

"You do not have to stay."

That statement angered him. "You know better than that. Of course I have to stay. This is a last-ditch fight for Shawcroft and Hardesty. If they let you live and if they let Hendricks and his family stay, they've lost their whole damn range."

All of them heard it in the silence that followed his words. A rumble in the ground, the pound of many hoofs. Prudence Dunson's face lost every vestige of color and Tate knew the sound reminded her of the one she'd heard as the men thundered into her yard the night her husband had been killed.

Hendricks didn't have to be told. He instantly blew out the lamp, leaving them in total darkness. Tate said, "Mrs. Dunson, you and Mrs. Hendricks go into the other room and get down on the floor. Hendricks, you and your boy take those two windows but don't show yourselves. I'll take the door."

As he spoke, he opened it. He knew he couldn't just fort up in the house with Hendricks and his son. At least ten men were riding into the yard. Maybe they were hired hands and maybe they'd balk at cold-blooded murder, but shooting into a darkened house was something at which they wouldn't balk.

It was almost a certainty that one or more of the occupants would be killed. Others would be wounded, and the thought of Prudence Dunson being shot was intolerable to Tate.

The shapes of the horsemen loomed

dark against the star-studded sky. Tate turned his head and whispered urgently, "Come bolt the door!" Without waiting to see if he would be obeyed, he sidled swiftly along the back wall of the house.

They saw his moving shape against the white frame wall. Shawcroft's voice roared, "There goes one of them! Get the son-of-a-bitch!"

Guns flashed. Tate dived for the corner, sliding. Bullets thudded into the building wall above him. He reached the corner, gathered hands and feet beneath him, and scrambled around it, hearing the pound of approaching hoofs.

Window glass shattered now and he heard the deep boom of a shotgun, which he supposed was Hendricks' gun. The horses, stung by birdshot, nickered with terror. They reared, some of them dumping their riders onto the ground.

In the confusion, Tate sprinted across the yard to the shed. He reached it without drawing fire, without being seen.

The invaders were in a cross fire now, and could be hurt, but unless the unforeseen happened it was just a matter of time until they killed Tate and wiped out all the occupants of the house.

Again the shotgun boomed. Again birdshot stung both invaders and their horses in the yard. Shawcroft's voice bawled, "Get that son-of-a-bitch with the shotgun!"

In another instant, Tate knew the house would be riddled. Close on the heels of Shawcroft's order, he snatched out his revolver and emptied it in the direction of the milling horsemen in the yard.

He was rewarded by one high yell of pain, and by the thrashings of a horse wounded severely enough to bring him crashing to the ground. Tate dropped to the ground in the doorway of the shed, rolled aside. A hail of bullets ripped the air where he had stood only an instant before.

Temporarily, at least, he had kept them from shooting into the house, but that respite wasn't going to last. Jamming his revolver back into its holster, he rolled back into the doorway, shoving his rifle out in front of him.

A bullet raked his back, bringing an instant rush of blood. Angered more than hurt, he fired at the flash.

Shawcroft and Hardesty shouted, almost as one, "There he is! Get him!"

Tate knew there was only one way this was going to be stopped. He had to get Shawcroft, or Hardesty, or both. Only if they were without leadership would the others be persuaded to stop.

Before they could open up on his muzzle flash, he rolled aside again. The guns outside sounded like a string of exploding firecrackers. Bullets gouged furrows in the dusty floor of the shed. Tate kept rolling until he was ten feet from the door. Then he got to his feet, glancing around for a way to get out of the shed.

It had only one door. But there was a window in the rear. He raced toward it, smashed it out with the butt of his rifle, trying to get all the glass but knowing he didn't have much time.

The sound of breaking glass brought another roar from Shawcroft out in front. "He's goin' out the back. Get around there and cut him off!"

Tate knew he'd never make it out the window now. But he had drawn them around to the back of the shed, which might leave the front unwatched.

In any case, he hadn't any choice. Bottled up here, it was only a matter of a minute or two before they riddled him. Running, building up speed as he crossed the shed, he headed for the door. He burst through it at top running speed.

He was halfway across the yard and into the midst of those who had remained in front before they realized what he had done. He collided with one man and knocked him rolling. He slammed his rifle stock squarely into another man's face and the man made a choked cry and sank to his knees, both hands going to his face.

At least, Tate thought fleetingly, while they were busy with him they weren't firing bullets into the house. Against the sky he caught a glimpse of the Confederate cavalry officer's hat that Hardesty always wore. Desperate, and knowing his time was running out, he raised his rifle and put a bullet squarely into the middle of Hardesty's chest. The man swayed a moment, then folded quietly to the ground.

Tate let out a roar. "Hardesty's dead! The rest of you will be too if you don't get the hell out of here!"

He thought those probably would be his last words. Surrounded in the open and a target for every man still on his feet, it could be no more than a matter of seconds before somebody succeeded in putting a bullet into him.

A shrill, woman's scream suddenly split the air. Tate couldn't tell whether the scream came from Prudence Dunson or Mrs. Hendricks, and he didn't have time to turn his head and look. He was seeking

Shawcroft, knowing only Shawcroft's death could now stop this fight.

A bullet took him in the thigh and he went crashing to the ground. Rolling, still unwilling to give up, he brought his rifle up and jacked another cartridge in. He bawled, "Shawcroft?"

He saw Shawcroft the instant that he yelled. Shawcroft stood less than ten feet away from him. Shawcroft's gun was pointed at him and in an instant its muzzle would explode. He tried to bring his own gun to bear but he seemed to be moving with agonizing slowness and knew he was going to be too late.

From a distance he seemed to hear the second scream. Pain from his wounded leg, which had at first been numb, now was shooting through him like a red-hot knife. His head reeled. He stared at Shawcroft standing there and waited for the flare of Shawcroft's gun.

But the flare came from a different direction, from the direction of the house. Shawcroft was flung back as if hit by a giant fist. Tate yanked his glance away, looked toward the bellow of the scatter gun.

He saw the blur of a woman's white dress, and instantly heard his own voice bawling, "Shawcroft's gone! Throw down your guns, all of you!"

The firing stopped as suddenly as it had begun. Tate sensed movement in the yard, the movement of those of the attackers who were able mounting their horses and riding away. Others remained, lying either wounded or dead upon the ground.

That blur, that light-colored woman's dress, came near to him and the woman knelt beside him. Her hand came out and touched his face, and her voice, soft and filled with terrible concern, asked, "How badly are you hurt, Mr. Tate?"

The tone of her voice answered the doubts he had felt earlier. He raised his own hand and closed it over hers and said, "Leg. I'll live. How about Hendricks and his wife and boy?"

Relief was overwhelming in Prudence Dunson's voice. "They are all right."

Tate struggled to get up. Her hands were strong as she helped him rise. She supported him on the wounded side and together they hobbled toward the house, in which a lamp now burned.

Sam Dunson was avenged, thought Tate. And now that he was, maybe Prudence could look forward once again, instead of back. His leg hurt like hell, but in spite of that Tate's mind was looking forward too.